PIRATES OF THE RANGE

Hell breaks loose when rustlers go on the prowl—a thousand head of cattle mysteriously vanish. Wylie Brooks and his partner Steve Tilton go on a hunt for justice that has a blazing outcome. These two Texas cowboys who had previously thought the Cathedral Butte country in Montana was cow heaven loosen up their guns...

Bertha Muzzy Bower, born in Cleveland, Minnesota, in 1871, was the first woman to make a career of writing Western fiction and remains one of the most widely known, having written nearly seventy novels. She became familiar with cowboys and ranch life at sixteen when her family moved to the Big Sandy area of Montana. She was nearly thirty and mother of three before she began writing under the surname of the first of her three husbands. Her first novel, *Chip, of the Flying U*, was initially published as a serial in 1904 and was an immediate success. Bower went on to write more books, fourteen in all, about the Flying U, one of the best being the short story collection, *The Happy Family*. In 1933 she turned to stories set prior to the events described in *Chip, of the Flying U*. *The Whoop-up* actually begins this saga, recounting Chip Bennett's arrival in Montana and at the Flying U. Much of the appeal of this saga is due to Bower's use of humor, the strong sense of loyalty and family depicted among her characters, as well as the authentic quality of her cowboys. She herself was a maverick who experimented with the Western story, introducing modern technologies and raising unusual social concerns—such as aeroplanes in *Skyrider* or divorce in *Lonesome Land*. She was sensitive to the lives of women on the frontier and created some extraordinary female characters, notably in Vada Williams in *The Haunted Hills*, Georgie Howard in *Good Indian*, Helen in *The Bellehelen Mine*, and Mary Allison in *Trouble Rides the Wind*, another early Chip Bennett story. She was also able to write Western novels memorable for the characterization of setting and dramatization of nature, such as *Van Patten* or *The Swallowfork Bulls*.

PIRATES OF THE RANGE

B. M. Bower

GUNSMOKE

First published by Collins

This hardback edition 2005
by BBC Audiobooks Ltd
by arrangement with
Golden West Literary Agency

ISBN 1 4056 8012 1

British Library Cataloguing in Publication Data available.

Printed and bound in Great Britain by
Antony Rowe Ltd., Chippenham, Wiltshire

Pirates of the Range

Chapter One: COW HEAVEN

IN NORTHERN MONTANA when the sun goes down in late September the air has a nip to it, just as a reminder that winter is on the way. Two riders silhouetted against a purple-and-crimson skyline felt the chill of coming night and shivered a little in their shirt sleeves as they reached for coats which the warmth of the day had caused them to shed.

The shorter of the two took a last long look across the grassy, red-walled coulee where the trail herd grazed hungrily after the long day's drive; mixed stock, the pick of the Roman Four's holdings in Texas, where most of the husky hard-muscled calves had been dropped.

In four months those cows, calves, heifers, and young steers had grazed across five states and territories and were well up toward the northern boundary line of the sixth. Mesquite, sagebrush, sand, rivers in flood, and creeks holding nothing but sunbaked rubble they knew. Times they had plodded with dust-caked eyelashes blinking against the glare, and lowed in mournful chant for water yet miles away. Times they had stood belly-deep and drunk their fill, moving out sluggishly at last to graze, the calves essaying a half-hearted attempt to gambol with awkward buck jumps in the unaccustomed lush green meadows.

When they struck the bunch-grass country their trail boss cannily turned them aside from the old Whoop-up Trail they had been following; he let them graze slowly northward like a band of sheep on home range. Water was plentiful, grass was curing down to the very roots, packed with nourishment, sweet as a ripe pecan nut.

No cattle had been lost in the short-grass country, few were footsore. Spread out on the flat, heads down as they fed, if they were not sleek neither were they showing too many ribs to the animal. For trail-herd cattle they were in good condition to face a winter in the North.

Perhaps the short man was thinking so as he shrugged into his coat, his horse standing quietly on the little ridge where the two had drawn rein. Half turning in the saddle he looked up at the steep, grass-covered butte at their backs; so steep and so high it was, one could imagine that it had been placed there deliberately by some forgotten pastoral god, a crude monument piled high to mark the quiet, sheltered valley below.

He turned again to that valley, saw stragglers in the creek plowing knee-deep to the bank, looked at his partner.

"Wylie, this sure looks to me like the place we've been hunting for." He drew in a long satisfied breath, let it go in the sigh of a tired man come home. "What yuh say we take possession, right here and now? We could travel till snow flies and not find anything better; nor as good, if you ask me."

He lifted an arm and pointed. "Look there, down

the creek. Timber enough to build with—cottonwood and box elder, and them's quakin' asp, back up that draw. And this coulee's got feed enough to winter every hoof we own. I took a *pasear* around the north side, awhile back. There ain't a sign of any stock been runnin' in here all summer. Grass, water, timber, and shelter—boy, them words spell cow heaven! And no one layin' any claim to it but God (where it says in the Bible, 'The earth is the Lord's and the fullness thereof'), and He ain't runnin' nothin' on it but rabbits and sage hens. What d'yuh say, Wylie? Do we tie onto this coulee for a ranch?"

"Suits me, down to the ground." Wylie, a tall young fellow with the limber grace of a born rider, leaned to slap a fly off the neck of his horse. "We drop our loop on 'er if you say so, Steve. I guess the cattle won't make any kick about it—or the boys, either."

"No, you bet your sweet life they won't!" Steve got out his papers and tobacco, laughed a little to himself, and stepped down off his horse to sit on a near-by rock and smoke in comfort while he viewed their new possessions and planned corrals, sheds, cabin, pointing and gesturing with wide sweeps of arm and letting his cigarette cool unheeded between his tobacco-stained fingers.

Beside him Wylie Brooks sat on his boot heels and listened, followed with long-lashed glances Steve's pointing fingers and nodded or spoke a sentence now and then as needful. While the long twilight held and their horses dozed they remained there weighing, sifting, adding a detail here, discarding one there as not immediately vital—building their spread in their minds and seeing just how it was going to look when it had been wrought with stout logs, poles, sod of the meadow soil for the roof over their heads, tamped earth for their floor.

In the coulee the cowboys rode here and there, rounding up the scattered herd, bedding them down on a knoll where the grass was belly-deep to the biggest calves, and the cows, full fed though they were, could not resist stopping to snatch a mouthful here and there. Close-grouped the herd stood, somnolently watching the night guard as they started their endless round, riding slowly, singing an old range song as they went. One by one the cattle lay down, sighing with repletion. In the cottonwood grove across the creek firelight twinkled.

Wylie rose to his feet, his fingers mechanically brushing down his thighs. "Meantime, I'm hungry as a she-wolf with a litter of pups," he observed in his pleasant drawl which tagged him as from the South. "Better come eat before you move into that house you've built."

"We'll move in, all right, and don't you forget it!" Steve laughed. "Got a life lease, direct from the Almighty Himself. Bet you what yuh dare, no white man that owns a cow has ever laid eyes on this coulee. If he had, he'd of glommed it right then and there."

"I never bet against a sure thing." Wylie lifted toe to stirrup, swung a leg over the cantle, and settled in the saddle with one motion and apparently no effort whatever. "If it wasn't so empty of stock sign, I'd say it's too good to be true, if you asked me."

Steve with his shorter legs heaved himself up with a grunt. "Hell, somebody has to discover things, don't they? No law against us bein' the ones, is they?"

"Not on your tintype. Only I'm not used to bein' this lucky. That's all."

Steve rode ten rods. "Well, dammit, you'll have to get used to it," he snorted tardily. "We're here first, and me, I'm located right now."

"Same here. Funny—I feel like an Israelite just landed in Canaan." Of a sudden Wylie pulled off his hat, slapped his horse down neck and shoulder with it and gave a shrill cowboy yip. "Bring on your milk and honey!" he yelled, and dug his heels into his galloping sorrel. *"Oh, Beulah land! Sweet Beulah land!"* He was singing at the top of his voice as he splashed through the shallow water and went tearing across the meadow to the gray tents and the firelight near the cottonwood grove.

Chapter Two: AN UNFRIENDLY CUSS

THAT IS HOW THE ROMAN FOUR OUTFIT, trailing north from the Texas line with Wylie Brooks and Steve Tilton sole owners of the herd, came to take possession of the coulee lying snug at the foot of Cathedral Butte and to call it home.

In those days there was little ceremony and less red tape connected with locating a cattle ranch in northern Montana. The land for the most part, especially in the more isolated regions, was virgin soil as yet unmarked by section corners or surveyors' stakes. As Steve had said, all outdoors lay there with its face turned to the sun and sky, with no one claiming it save God and Uncle Sam, and neither seeming in the mood to press that claim.

Uninhabited—save by a few wandering remnants of Indian tribes, a few scattered buffalo (also the remnants of vast herds that had roved the plains not so long ago), a few wolves and coyotes, fewer white men —there it lay, waiting for whoever chose to call it his own.

With the days growing short and the nights nippy, they did not wait to discover what might lie to the north of them—whether more and better wilderness or some mark of civilization creeping westward. Time pressed. The Roman Four outfit bestirred themselves at work to which they were none too well accustomed.

Hands used to the feel of rope and branding-iron grew blisters under the rub of axe handles. Lariats, stretched with the weight of fighting steer and braced cow pony, now dragged close to the ground, snaking out logs for the cabin and sheds, poles for corrals.

Cutting and shaping trees into logs, laying them up in stout walls, sawing out windows and doors, laying the roof and covering it deep with rich loam from the grove where they built—all these things they did well because the winter storms would be a bitter test of their handiwork and betray slipshod building. Because they hated all work they could not perform from the back of a horse, and the sooner they were through the better they would be pleased, they worked fast. Shelter they must have. All right, hop to it and get it over with! But for choice, they would rather trail a herd five hundred miles across alkali flats than build one forty-foot corral.

Thus the cottonwood grove on the little knoll beside

the creek blossomed swiftly into ranch buildings. Not a man rode beyond the confines of the coulee until the building was done to the last shed, buttressed against the stable for warmth and economy of logs and labor.

Winter was creeping down from the high country to the north, indeed was almost upon them, when their task was done; and still the men of the Roman Four knew no more of what lay beyond than on the day of their arrival.

Then, one Sunday, Wylie Brooks made his toilsome way to the crest of Cathedral Butte. He did not even know that it was called Cathedral Butte. The boys of the Roman Four spoke of it succinctly as "Big Butte"— which it certainly was when viewed from the coulee gouged into its base. From the top Wylie gazed out over a rugged expanse of ridges and deep canyons, with here and there a broader coulee somewhat similar to their own. Far beyond all that, he glimpsed a wide streak of gray which he knew was a river, and having a fair idea of the general topography of the country he guessed at once that there lay the Missouri.

It was great to stand high above this unpeopled world. Brown grass lay thickly matted upon its precipitous slopes, like a wool blanket flung down over the peak by some housewifely goddess. He could almost fancy that he saw the huge blanket whipping gently in the crisp wind that blew across the crest. Here and there black outcroppings of rock thrust out through the grass, making jagged holes in the smooth expanse.

Steep as was the butte's high slopes, thin precarious cow trails angled in long switchbacks to the top. Occasionally these intrepid trails skirted sheer drops of a hundred feet or more. Again they sidled past concave declivities where the grass was slippery as glare ice. The range cattle knew. Following those trails, a horse could make it to the very top, provided his wind held out; how he would get back down was something else which he'd have to figure for himself—or his rider for him.

But these were casual thoughts drifting through Wylie's mind and gone again. Always his eyes returned to that tumbled waste below him which he knew was "the Badlands," where generous fertility of soil lay within hand's grip of barren stretches that held nothing save what red clay and yellow sandstone would grudgingly yield. And that was little enough to starve a rabbit.

To a man who had lived most of his life on bald prairie and level plain where the vision is bounded by curved skyline, like the ocean, this savage mingling of wild grass meadows and sterile soil, of grim cliffs and sheltered valley, held the fascination of novelty. Devilish country to lose cattle in, but he liked it just the same. All right when a fellow got to know all the twists and turns, he reckoned.

As he was making his way back down the butte's easiest side he saw a horseman riding down off a ridge to the north, apparently heading straight for the butte. Save the Roman Four outfit, it was the first human being Wylie had seen since they had located here. Partly from curiosity, but also because he would not turn aside from the trail he had planned to take back to his horse, Wylie kept on going.

At the base of the steepest slope, down which he had dug heels to keep from sliding, he met the stranger face to face, the rider coming up out of a little draw. It was evident then that he had seen Wylie on the butte and had taken a short cut to meet him. A little, ginger-whiskered man well past middle age, he was, a man with cold gray eyes that looked guardedly out at his world from beneath bushy eyebrows a shade lighter than his beard. Just now those eyes were about as friendly as two bullets.

"Hello, stranger," Wylie called cheerfully, checking his advance with some skill. "Coming to make a Sunday call?"

"Might be—and then agin, I might not. Just ridin' around. Where might you hail from, young feller?"

"Where I hail from is a long way from here, old timer. But just to be neighborly, I'll say I'm located right around the nose of this butte and down the coulee a ways. We're the Roman Four outfit; trailed a herd up from the South. Them's our cattle taking life easy down there along the creek." Wylie pulled a thumb from inside his belt and waved a negligent hand that still failed to conceal honest pride in the spread.

"Humph." Ginger-Whiskers eyed him speculatively. "Must be damn recent, your comin' into this coulee and makin' yourself to home thataway. Couple of my boys was ridin' over this way, too, three weeks ago, and they never said a word about the Lightnin' havin' new neighbors so close by."

"Three weeks ago is when we pulled in here. Fine grass country, this. We didn't know we had neighbors anywhere close, but she's a big old country, and I don't reckon it'll be crowded for years to come. Any place nearer than Fort Benton, or Billings, where we can get winter supplies? And we're needing horse feed right bad, too. Or we will, later on."

"Kismet's right acrost the river from my place. Pike Stoddard's my name. Run the Lightnin' brand." The horseman squinted and spat off to one side of his horse. "You can git most anything in the line of grub at Kismet—if you ain't too dainty in your wants. Horse feed's another proposition. Maybe the KM, down river from Kismet, could let you have some. Or the Block Diamond."

"You couldn't, I reckon?"

Pike Stoddard gave him a sharp glance. "I'm short as it is," he said tersely.

"Well, I sure am obliged for the information, any-way," Wylie told him, and meant it in all sincerity. "We've been so busy building and getting ready for winter that we haven't prospected around yet looking for neighbors." He turned and glanced back up the butte. "I climbed the pinnacle to see what the country looked like." He grinned companionably.

"Hunh. Suit you any?" The old man was studying him with quick, sharp glances that seemed to take Wylie's measure from many angles.

"Plenty wild," Wylie shrugged. "But I'll say it suits me down to the ground."

" 'Cause it's wild?"

"Well, it's plenty roomy, and I like that. I only said it *looks* wild, Mr. Stoddard. May not be when you get to know it."

"Looks," Stoddard vouchsafed, studying a half plug

of tobacco as if trying to decide where to set his teeth, "looks is deceivin', they say. In this case they ain't. The closer yuh git, the wilder it is."

Just what he meant by that Wylie did not know. His horse whinnied twice, just around the tapered shoulder of the bluff, and he moved toward it—Ginger-Whiskers, as he mentally called Stoddard, following close behind. The man wasn't friendly—nor was he definitely hostile. Guarded neutrality, Wylie thought, would describe his tone and manner very well. As Wylie mounted the tall black and could face his visitor on a level, his obligation as host suddenly occurred to him.

"Better come on down to the house, Mr. Stoddard, and get acquainted with my pardner, Steve Tilton. White a man as you'll ever meet. And it's getting along suppertime. We've got a Mexican cook that can make a slab of sowbelly taste like chicken, and his *frijoles* are something to remember. Better come. Steve'll be glad to meet you."

Pike Stoddard looked down the coulee to where the new log buildings huddled in the cottonwood grove. He leaned and spat in that direction.

"I hate a Mexican worse'n a rattlesnake," he stated with cold finality. "I wouldn't eat after a greaser if I was starvin'. How many men you got?"

"Twelve—and the cook makes thirteen."

"Thirteen's an unlucky number; know that? How many more greasers in the outfit?"

"Oh, we're all greasers and Yaqui Indians, Mr. Stoddard," Wylie assured him blandly. "Sure you don't like *frijoles* well enough to try ours?"

"No, I'll be gittin' back. G'day." And Pike Stoddard turned his gray pacer and rode off the way he had come.

Until Stoddard's black hat-crown dipped behind the ridge and no more was to be seen of it, Wylie sat holding in his horse with a tight rein and watched. What he expected not even he could have told. Though his right hand rested on his thigh within easy reach of his gun, he was not thinking consciously of any danger to himself. Pike Stoddard had neither looked behind him nor troubled to put himself out of sight quickly, as he could have done easily in the gully. Instead, he had crossed the gully and ridden straight up the slope beyond, and over the ridge, as perfect a target as an enemy could want. He wasn't afraid of being shot in the back, that much was certain.

An unfriendly cuss, though. And that was how Wylie described the old man to Steve afterward: a dried-up little runt who carried a chip on his shoulder and went out of his way to be ornery, but was possibly honest enough in his way—at least he didn't seem to be a bit uneasy about himself. Slap a man in the face about having Mexicans in his outfit, and then turn and ride off cool as a cucumber.

"He can ride to hell, for all me," Steve snorted. "But that news about Kismet, down on the river, sure is welcome. If that's straight goods, Wylie, we've got nothing to worry about. We can winter fine, and we don't care what kind of neighbors we've got."

A rash statement, as Steve must have admitted to himself later if he remembered having made it—which he probably did not.

Chapter Three: SIZING UP KISMET

KISMET LOOMED LARGE IN THEIR MINDS next morning.
Wylie wanted to find out for himself how truthful a
man old Ginger-Whiskers would prove to be; they
both were curious to see and size up the place and
solve if they could the problem of horse feed for the
winter ahead. Another summer, and they would have
plenty of hay put up for their saddle stock. This winter the horses would have to forage for grass, probably
under snow at that, and only grain would keep them
in condition for riding.

And riding there would be, plenty of it, to keep the
cattle from drifting south before the storms of winter.
Let them once drop their calves on this new range and
they would call it home, but for the next few months
they would need watching, and that meant good horses
would be a necessity. Few of the men knew anything
about Montana winters, save what they had been told.
It would never do to start riders out on weak mounts
in this rough country. Grain the Roman Four must
have at any price.

Wylie had neglected to ask how far it was to Kismet,
or whether they might hope to find a wagon road
leading to the town. Therefore he and Steve were in
their saddles at the first crack of dawn, and they led
behind them two pack-horses which would carry supplies; the grain would come later—they hoped.

Finding Kismet proved after all a simple matter.
Riding up the coulee to the butte, they trailed Pike
Stoddard to his lair—which meant coming within sight

of the Lightning corrals and stables. He had a very competent-looking spread, Wylie conceded, but they did not stop for a neighborly call. Kismet they could see—part of it, at least—just across the river. There was what looked like a ford, with a wagon road leading into it. There was also a ferry of sorts. The ferry they knew they could cross on, if they had to, Steve had observed, but why pay out good money if the ford was safe? Teams had crossed just lately, by the tracks.

"So the old pelican didn't lie to me, after all," Wylie remarked as they splashed into the river. "You know, I thought all the time he was stringing me along. Judging by his looks and actions, he's plumb mean and I wouldn't put anything past him. Wonder if there's something scaly about Kismet? Thieves and cutthroats, do you reckon?"

Steve laughed at him. "Can't you let a poor old man tell the truth if he wants to? He don't have to be purty and sweet to be truthful, does he?"

Wylie's head moved sidewise, and he was not smiling. "Just the same, there was a look in his eye when he talked about Kismet," he said reflectively. Then he laughed. "Well, shucks! I don't reckon he's liked any too well over here," he decided. "That's probably it. Soon as I size up the town I'll know for sure."

Sizing up Kismet proved to be a matter of one glance. As a town it failed ignobly to live up to its designation. For Kismet was entirely comprised of one long, low store building apparently crammed with supplies for a thinly settled country. Attached to the store building was a longer, lower structure built impartially of logs, slabs, and rock from the river bottom.

This, they gathered, was hotel and saloon; either or both, according to one's needs and desires.

The proprietor of this all-purpose establishment was a big, red-faced, jolly man with a friendly voice and a laugh that made the world a happy-go-lucky place for the moment. His name, they soon discovered, was Bill Longbow; Big Bill, someone called him, and the big man answered as if he was used to the cognomen. Bill Longbow, as Steve afterward remarked, was the town of Kismet. There wasn't any more.

As strangers in the city, they knew well what was expected of them. They therefore kept walking until they stood before the saloon bar, and with a hospitable gesture called everyone up for a drink with them. That ceremony having been performed with due decorum, they proceeded to make themselves agreeable, careful to ask no rash questions and at the same time to satisfy any lingering curiosity in the minds of the natives. Particularly in the mind of Big Bill Longbow.

Stragglers drifted in, loitered casually on some small errand, drifted out again. Bill Longbow knew them all, hailed them as friends, apparently dismissed them completely from his mind the moment they passed through his door. To Steve and Wylie he now and again offered some enlightening comment:

"Freighter. Good man, when he stays sober. . . . That feller owns a nice little mine, back up here in the Belt mountains. Looks like he's about to strike it rich— only that wouldn't be the way the cards fall, when I grubstake a man. I'm unlucky that way. Grubstake every lousy rock-tapper in the country that ain't worth the powder to blow him to hell, and when a good man comes along— Still, I dunno—kinda begins to look as if Pat Mullen (feller just went out) is liable to make me some money and change my luck." He laughed a rich, throaty chuckle. "Anybody but me, I'd say it's a cinch."

A tall, good-looking young man with the stilted, spring-kneed walk of a rider came in, glanced at them sidelong as he walked up to the counter, pushing back his gray range hat as he came to a stand. Bill Longbow crooked a finger at the Roman Four men and nodded. "Dave, I want you to meet some new neighbors, just moved in with a bunch of Texas cattle. Brooks and Tilton, runnin' the Roman Four brand. Boys, this here is Dave Spellman, owner of the K.M."

The three shook hands, Longbow smiling almost paternally upon them as he watched, arms braced far apart on the counter.

"I can let you have oats, all right," Longbow continued the discussion which Dave Spellman's entrance had interrupted, "but if you want hay to winter your horses, Dave's the man you'll have to talk to. And if he charges you more than the going price, just let me know and I'll stick him on the price of flour. Learn him to be fair and honest." He laughed with the others, drawing down his fat eyelids until his eyes were almost hidden.

"How about it, Dave?" he sobered to ask. "These boys can give a good account of themselves—I had quite a little talk with 'em. They come in here to locate, and help build up the country. Got a nice bunch of cattle, seems like, and couple hundred head of horses. . . . Me, I'm tickled to death to see the right kinda men come in here to live. Helps us poor devils that much, that has to depend on selling grub to settlers, to make a living. I tell yuh—"

"Don't give us that old song and dance, Bill." Dave Spellman laughed in his face. "Why, you old highbinder, the prices you charge, you could buy out all us poor cattlemen for cash and never miss it. You make a living! That's a good one!"

This, Wylie surmised, was merely a little friendly badinage exchanged for their own amusement. Both men were laughing.

"We sure would like to buy hay if we can get it," he said, passing over their pleasantries with each other. "That is, if the price ain't too steep, and we can get it into our coulee—over by that big butte—without packing it in."

Longbow straightened and looked businesslike. "How about that, Dave? You got more hay'n you need, ain't yuh? I'm willin' to let you handle a little of their money, so long as you leave 'em enough to buy their grub from me." He was chuckling again. "Don't you go to work and rob 'em, like you did me, last ten ton I bought."

Dave Spellman grinned and lowered an eyelid gently for the benefit of the strangers. "You'd beller like a calf at weaning time if I charged them any less, you old hypocrite," he retorted before he turned to Wylie and Steve. "I can let you have a few tons, I guess. If you get skinned, it'll be this same Bill Longbow who's the guilty party. He's had his own way here too long, if you ask me. Wait till you start laying in your winter grub, and you'll see!"

"Now, Dave, that ain't no way to do—try and drive custom away from me! I got to live, and so has Dolly. You want me to give stuff away and starve her?"

"Not so you could notice." Dave's tone sobered in spite of his laugh. He swung about with his back to the counter and began to roll a cigarette while he looked these two new neighbors over more carefully, with straight, not-too-searching glances that met their own gaze frankly, not ashamed of his curiosity.

"You came kinda late in the season, didn't yuh? Texas cattle don't take kindly to Montana winters; not if they're slammed right into cold weather without getting used to it gradual."

It was Steve who answered. "We thought some of settling in the Platte River country. But the winters there are about as cold as here, they told us, and too many herds have been turned loose there. We lost time getting here, but the cattle's in good shape and we struck a big wide coulee, back here a few miles, that is a dandy, all right. Lots of shelter, best grass I ever saw in my life—ain't been a hoof in it all summer, till we trailed in. I reckon they'll winter all right. It's the saddle horses we've got to worry about. Unless," he glanced up, grinning a little, "we can make a deal on some hay."

Chapter Four: STEVE IS HARD HIT

CROSS-LEGGED, DAVE SPELLMAN LEANED BACK against the bar and smoked thoughtfully while he listened. "You're back in there by Cathedral Butte, I take it. In Cottonwood Coulee." He shot a quick sidelong glance at Longbow and knocked the ash from his cigarette. "Peacherino of a place, all right. But it's a long haul from my stacks. . . . You're not such a long way from the Lightning. Have you tried Pike Stoddard? He's got more hay than I have—"

"Stoddard told me yesterday he didn't have any to spare," Wylie told him, and instantly sensed a change in the atmosphere.

"Told yuh that, did he?" the big storekeeper cut in. "He cuts more hay'n anybody in the country. The old—" He checked himself. "Oh, well, never mind. I ain't goin' to read no man's pedigree behind his back. You'll soon find him out for yourself. Call on yuh, yet?"

"Not exactly. I met him over at the Butte, yesterday. He didn't come on to camp, though."

"Musta been daylight," chuckled Longbow, and gave Spellman a quick look.

"Oh, don't go hinting things you can't prove, Bill," Dave mildly remonstrated. "Old Pike may be ornery as the devil, and he may have some ways that don't exactly jibe with the Good Book. But you don't *know* as much as you suspect." He tossed his cigarette stub upon the littered stove hearth and looked at the Roman Four men.

"My cousin Dick works for the Lightning," he explained. "And while I must admit I haven't got much time for Dick, I'm here to say he wouldn't throw in with any outfit that was doing rusty work. If I thought for a minute any cousin of mine—" He stopped, his teeth striking together with a click.

"Nobody said anything against your cousin," Bill

Longbow expostulated hastily. "Don't go flying off the handle—"

With a sharp gesture of his hand, young Spellman silenced Bill. "You may as well know—you'll find it out soon enough." His clouded gaze held Steve's and Wylie's eyes upon him. "We've been bothered considerable in these Badlands with what looks like rustlers' work. Nobody seems to be able to know where to pin it. I don't believe in accusing anyone till I've got proof to back it up.

"Bill Longbow, here, don't own any cattle, so he hasn't lost any. You might say he takes what the college sharps call an academic interest in everything that doesn't concern his store or his saloon. Bill says whatever comes into that alleged mind of his, without fear or favor. You mustn't pay any attention to him. He's kind of a privileged character around here. Takes out a gover'ment license every spring and fall to shoot off his mouth regardless. Nobody takes Bill serious."

"Oh, they don't, ay?" Bill snarled with bitter humor. "Just the samey, I'd ruther be on my side of the river than old Pike's, if I was runnin' any cattle." Longbow moved ponderously from behind the counter as a bell clanged outside. "Dinner's ready. Come on and eat, boys. On the house."

At the table, with his plate and his mouth full, Bill reverted to the argument over Pike Stoddard. "Dave's right. You don't want to mind what I say. I got a grudge agin Pike Stoddard, and some of these days I'll git him where the hair's short!"

"Now, Bill, you know you don't mean all that."

"Hell, I mean more'n half of it, anyway." Big Bill

gave a short laugh. "Pike Stoddard's the stingiest man
I ever see. Why, he hauls all his supplies clear in from
Billings, ruther than trade with me! What reason have
I got for likin' that old coot? Any man that'll see a
thrivin' emporium of trade set right across the river
from him and starve, while he hauls grub in from the
outside, had oughta be run outa the country. Why, old
Pike ain't wet a hoof in that ford since Hector was a
pup—and I don't know who Hector was, and don't
give a damn."

"Well, it sure looks like the Roman Four had better
patronize home industry," Steve laughed. "If you always sell as good grub as you put on the table, Mr.
Longbow, my horse's hoofs'll never be dry."

"Takin' that stand, you're a gentleman and you can
start right in callin' me Bill. Both of yuh. I'm proud
to have you in the country, and I won't never charge
you more'n double what a thing costs me laid down
here. All I want is an honest livin'." His big bulk
shook with his mirth.

Wylie wondered just how much—if any—of Big Bill
Longbow's remarks should be taken seriously. The
twinkle in Bill's eyes belied his hardest words. Yet
Wylie gathered that Pike Stoddard was not his favorite
neighbor, and that there was some undercurrent of
feeling against the Lightning outfit throughout the
country. Dave Spellman had practically admitted it.

They lingered late into the evening and crossed the
river with Dave Spellman, leading their pack-horses
well loaded with provisions. There was a passable road,
Dave told them, coming into the coulee's mouth and
crossing the small river—Skunk Creek, he called it. It

was not a road much used, and the Roman Four would find the trail over to the Lightning ranch a short-cut to Kismet for saddle horses.

He'd get ten tons of hay hauled over to their place before it stormed, if he could. South of the river he had a line camp, and several stacks of hay. If they had teams and wagons, and could do their own hauling, he'd lend them hay racks and make a cut on the price. He would rather do that, he said, because his outfit was pretty busy right now. He'd tell the boys in camp to fix them up with what they wanted.

When they separated a few miles south of the ford, young Spellman pointed the way for them. It was plain enough. They could not miss it in that bright moonlight, he assured them.

"And that's the best job we've done since we struck this country," Steve observed as they rode on through the wide brushy draws where faint indications of a wagon trail guided them toward their own coulee, and Cathedral Butte, as they knew it now, bulked high against the stars to mark the end of their journey. "We know what kinda neighbors we got, and that means everything in a wide open country like this. Fine folks as you'd want to meet anywhere."

"Couldn't have picked a better spot, if you ask me," Wylie agreed. "Easy riding distance to a trading-post— you'll be makin' that trip regular from now on, I reckon," he added slyly.

"I shore would admire to know what put that idea into your fool head," Steve retorted testily.

"You admire right out loud with your eyes, Steve. I saw Big Bill Longbow watching you sideways. You look out, boy. Dolly's too pretty a girl not to have a string of beaux a mile long. And Big Bill is going to be damn choosy about a son-in-law, if I have sized him up right—and I think I have."

"You talk too much with your mouth," Steve snubbed him. But he rode dreamily along with his hands clasped on the saddle horn, staring straight ahead at the moonlighted wilderness before them. He had not spoken a dozen words to Dolly Longbow, but it was perfectly apparent to his partner that he was hard hit. He proved it further by flaring abruptly:

"A man with any brains or heart ought to know better than to settle down beside a freight trail when he's got womenfolks in the family. . . . And if he does, he's got no business putting any daughter of his to waiting on all the riffraff that comes to buy a meal off him."

"If you ask me, Big Bill Longbow would wing an angel outa the sky and put her to slingin' hash, if he thought it would draw trade," Wylie replied cynically. "Good-natured and big-hearted as they come—but he keeps one eye on the almighty dollar. You can gamble on that. I sure do like Dave Spellman, though. I'm glad he's the one we're buying hay from."

To this Steve answered with a preoccupied grunt, and after that they rode in silence.

Chapter Five: TELLTALE CARCASSES

THAT WINTER PASSED QUIETLY ENOUGH and very much as the Roman Four owners had anticipated that it would. During the first couple of months the line riders had been out on all sides of the coulee, holding the cattle within its borders. But with sheltered basins and grass-bottomed canyons scattered all through the Badlands, it soon began to seem foolish to hold the more venturesome animals from foraging farther afield. They would range all through these hills next season, anyway, and they seemed contented enough in some tucked-away gulch. So the line-riding was done to the south of the coulee and butte, guarding against any of the stock trying to drift back toward their own range.

With the horses it was the same. Those not to be ridden for a week or more were left to range where they pleased, the line riders on the south boundary of the range pushing back any homesick drifters.

Besides the small incidents of line riding, nothing broke the monotony save an occasional ride to Kismet, or riding down to the KM line camp where several riders stayed, or a visit from Dave Spellman and other men of the KM outfit. The Block Diamond, ranging farther down the river on the Kismet side, below the KM headquarters, came less often to Cathedral Butte. As for the Lightning, they held no intercourse whatever with Pike Stoddard and his men. Old Pike they had met once or twice on the trail, said hello, and let it go at that. Lightning riders they knew only by the jagged brand on their mounts.

Taking the winter as a whole, the Roman Four was content with life and their choice of a location up north. Pleasures were few, but these were men of simple tastes who could spend hours and much labor over the rawhide riatas they fashioned during the long cold evenings, and find pleasure in the work, or in wrangling with heavy witticisms over a game of cards, or swapping hair-lifting tales of adventure with the KM boys when they rode over for a visit. Even literature had its devotees, a stack of pamphlet-printed romances having been borrowed from the KM by one of the boys, who rode home with twenty pounds of *Fireside Library* books (three and five cents each), wrapped in a gunny sack and tied behind the cantle: *The Count of Monte Cristo, Pickwick Papers, Madcap Violet,* and *She Stoops to Conquer* among the lot.

Only Steve was given to moods of morose silence as winter walked with the nipping steps of short days toward the long free stride of whooping spring winds and thundering rain. Steve Tilton was a goner, according to Wylie, from the moment when he looked up and took his first cup of coffee from Dolly Longbow's hand. Not a week went by without Steve Tilton's finding some excuse for riding to Kismet.

And that was all right with Wylie and the boys, so far as it went. Given the opportunity and a little encouragement, no doubt any one of the dozen would have fallen in love with Dolly. It just happened to be Steve who had widened his loop for her first, and by the unwritten law of their kind, other Roman Four eligibles reined aside from the girl and gave Steve a clear run for his money.

Clear run so far as they were concerned. But there was another man in the race and riding hard, as Steve discovered during Christmas week. That he happened to be a Lightning man, and none other than Dave Spellman's cousin Dick, did not help matters any so far as Steve was concerned. He began to hate the entire

Lightning outfit with an unreasoning bitterness, and he even carried his grudge to Dave because he chanced to be Dick's cousin.

Steve was not too easy to live with in peace, those days.

On a raw day in early March he and Wylie rode out together to round up a bunch of saddle horses that had taken to ranging west of the Butte where the creek that watered the coulee had its source in a long narrow basin fed with warm springs.

On the bare ridges the wind had a bite of frost when they faced it, but in the deep sheltered places where the sun lay warm on the brown grass there was a shy promise of crocuses soon to thrust blue cups above the grass on their brown furry stems. And there was here and there a hint of green among the grass roots, and once when they rode quietly across a sun-drenched knoll a few venturesome prairie dogs chip-chip-chipped shrewishly and then ducked head first into their burrows, pert little tails wiggling like thumbed noses as the horsemen passed in silence.

Let this weather hold, and the meadow larks would soon be singing their melodious snatches of song, and the curlews would gravely inquire, *Cor-reck? Cor-reck?* as they sailed low overhead trailing their long pink legs behind them. By this and by that, spring would be here in another two or three weeks.

To Wylie, who had held himself sternly aloof from romantic entanglements, the world was good and the day was fine; he rode his top horse, which walked with a spring in all four feet. He whistled as he faced the wind and the sun, pulled up to laugh at the prairie dogs, and generally comported himself as a young man does whose mind is carefree.

Though he did really feel that way, he was emphasizing his mood a little in the hope of prying Steve out of his own private slough of despond without resorting to words, which would probably be highly resented. Steve had come in late from Kismet the night before, and he had rolled out of his bunk late that morning looking black as a thunderhead. He had cussed Juan in Mex because the coffee was not at boiling-point when it was poured, and he had not spoken one word in more than an hour of riding.

By all these signs and portents Wylie judged that something had gone radically wrong with Steve's visit in Kismet. Maybe the two suitors had come together and locked horns; maybe Steve had popped the question and been handed his walking-papers—maybe there had been a lovers' quarrel or something. Whatever it was, Steve could, in Wylie's opinion, give a she-bear with the bellyache some pointers in general ugliness that morning. Conversation was best omitted if possible.

But as they topped a low ridge Wylie forgot his vow of silence. "What's that, down there in that hollow?" He gestured. "Looks like the wolves have pulled down some critter. Two or three, for that matter. Let's go take a look, Steve."

Without answering, Steve reined his horse around and they rode down the steep slope to the place, their horses squatting and half sliding, unable to gain a foothold. In the narrow gully several carcasses lay sprawled in the yellow sunlight. As they approached, a coyote jumped from behind one heap and went streaking for the nearest shelter.

Side by side, eyes taking in every detail, the two rode close to the first red heap and pulled in their snorting horses.

Wylie leaned and peered, drew his eyebrows together, rode around to the other side and bent to peer again. He straightened, glanced at the other mutilated carcasses near by, and back to the thing at his horse's uneasy feet.

"Well, I'm—*damned!*"

Wolves had been at work, but wolves had not done the killing. With every animal it was the same: head and front quarters mauled by the wolves, and nothing but shriveled hide where the hind quarters should have been.

"Butchered, and the hind quarters packed off! It's— you there the other night when Dave was telling us boys about this same thing happening up north of the river? It's the same identical trick that was played on the Flying U, up north." Wylie's eyes were hard and angry. "Come on, Steve. Let's look 'em over for the brand—if the damn' skunks left any."

Together they dismounted and examined the first carcass. From there they went on down the gully, taking each in turn. The brands were there, impudently left for all to see. In every hide was branded the big IV on the left ribs—their own brand.

In complete silence the two looked at each other, then turned away to mount and ride.

"I'd give a lot to know who did all that," Wylie said at last, speaking through set teeth. The muscles along his jaw had lumped and hardened.

"If you want to know what I think, I say the Lightning done it." Steve's tone held a sour satisfaction, as if he would be glad enough to come to grips with their nearest neighbor.

"It might be, but Pike Stoddard don't strike me as being that big a fool. If he was smart, he'd pick on cattle farther away from home."

"Not if it's a new outfit and he wants to drive 'em out—or build a fight and kill 'em off."

"Well, better not say anything to the boys till we know something for sure," Wylie cautioned. "Let's take a look around back in the hills, Steve."

Side by side they rode up the slope of the next ridge, toward the Lightning range, and down into the gully beyond. Here they found a few more carcasses—and the brand was the Roman Four.

In another deeper basin they counted twelve carcasses, unmistakably butchered as the others had been. They did not take the trouble to ride down and inspect the brands, they felt so certain they knew.

"The Flying U, up north by the Bear Paws, was a new outfit, too, when the same thing happened to them," Wylie observed significantly. "Dave was telling me about 'em a month or so ago. Seems they went to work and cleaned out that neck of the woods—killed off a few rustlers and made it a good country up there. It don't seem possible anybody'd try to work the same scheme on us."

The boldness of the outrage staggered them, left them stunned and helpless. There had not been the slightest attempt at concealment of the crime. Easy as it would have been to cut out the brand and leave the ownership of the butchered cattle in doubt, not one had been removed or even defaced in any way. It seemed as though the rustlers had deliberately planned to show their contempt for these strangers in the country. It was a challenge, nothing less. The Roman Four could like it or they could lump it.

All that afternoon the two owners of the butchered cattle rode through the hills north and west of the ranch—two directions which none of the line riders had bothered to cover, since homesick cattle would be sure to drift south and east to the open country. In some sheltered nooks there were several carcasses scattered here and there; in others cattle fed quietly with no sign of having been molested.

When they finally turned their horses' heads toward home they had counted over fifty telltale heaps of hide and bones, some half eaten by wolves and coyotes, others untouched. And they knew that some of the butchering had been done within the last few nights— or days, since the marauders were so bold.

Even Wylie had little to say on that homeward ride. There was little profit in bewailing their loss or in making threats. They were being robbed, deliberately and by wholesale methods, and whoever the robbers were they had made it plain to their victims that they did not fear the consequences.

Chapter Six: SECRET ENEMY

IN A LAND AS YET UNFENCED, lying open and free as the winds that blew across it, cattlemen counted their range by the natural boundaries of rivers or mountains which barred further wanderings of their cattle. There was grazing for as many cattle as they owned, and they made it a point to own as many as they could set their brands upon—legally as a rule, though that rule was not always followed implicitly.

Among those who numbered their cattle in thousands the Roman Four was rated a very small outfit. Three thousand head was just a nice little start, which with luck and patience—mostly luck—might in time grow to a real spread. It was the contemptuous boldness of the rustlers that rankled deepest in the minds of Wylie Brooks and Steve Tilton. That, and the thought that since the rustlers killed beef with no pretense of caution, there was no telling what more they would do.

Probably the most intolerable phase of the plundering was not the loss of the cattle so much as their lost sense of security. It was the fact that this new country which they had begun to call home held an enemy as secret as he was unscrupulous. True, Steve named the Lightning. But there was not the faintest shred of evidence that Pike Stoddard knew anything about it. Mere suspicion was not enough. What they needed was proof, which would give them the right to defend themselves.

"Well, whoever done it, they sure as hell never got outside all that meat themselves," Steve broke their long and gloomy silence. "Somebody's been haulin' out beef and sellin' it. It ain't likely we found half the critters that's been butchered. And right in them few gullies we counted close to fifty—do you realize what that amounts to, Wylie?"

"You're damn' right I do. It looks to me like that beef-butchering gang that worked north of the river awhile back had crossed over this side when they got smoked out up there. They may be the ones that's been rustling cattle in through these hills. Dave told me he's been bothered a lot, the last season or two; but I gathered it was calves mostly that the KM lost. He never mentioned any beef butchering. I think I'll ride over and see if they've run across any—"

"You take my advice, Wylie, and don't say a word about this to anybody." Steve turned in his saddle so that he faced his partner. "Recollect, we're strangers in this part of the world. When you come right down to it, we don't know none of 'em, not to really know 'em. My doctrine is to trust nobody till he's been tested out and proved."

Steve revealed nothing. "You mind what I tell you, and don't spill this to a soul outside our own outfit. We'll put the boys wise, and just lay low for a while."

"Well, that's all right with me. Only, I'd tell Dave Spellman and see what he thinks or knows."

"What he thinks about it won't put them fifty and more critters back up on their feet, Wylie. You wait. If Dave Spellman's got anything on his mind, let him be the one to start talkin'. Keep it in our own outfit, I say. We're lucky we ain't got a man in the outfit but what come up the trail with us. We know our own boys. We know their pedigrees. There won't be any spies among 'em, that's a cinch. And if we tell 'em all to keep their mouths shut, all hell couldn't pry a word out of their teeth. We won't be double-crossed, you can bank on that."

"Dave Spellman wouldn't double-cross us, either. He's got no more use for the Lightning—"

"Maybe he ain't. That ain't the point I'm gettin' at. S'pose you told Dave, and he told one or two of his boys, and word got around. You'd blame him for spreadin' it, wouldn't yuh? Well, I say, keep this bottled up right inside our own bunch. Then if it gets out before we're ready, we'll go down the line and have a housecleanin'."

Wylie studied him curiously. This was more like the old Steve of last fall, before they took that first ride to Kismet. "Well, what's your plan? Why all the secrecy?" he demanded at last.

"Just this—and we don't want to take any chance of a slip-up. We can see this thing through alone if we play our hands right. What I want to do is find out who's been hauling beef outa the country. If you ask me, Wylie, right there is the key to the hull damn combination."

"We ought to be able to find that out from Bill Longbow, easy enough. He keeps cases on every dollar in the country, especially if it shows any signs of turning over. Why don't you ride in tonight, Steve, and see what you can find out?"

"Why don't you go yourself?" Steve growled. "You don't have to think up errands for me, old timer."

But Wylie shied off from that opening. "I'm no match for Big Bill Longbow," he declared. "I like the old devil, and first thing I knew I'd be unburdening all my troubles to him. He seems too many different kinds of men, and he talks too much. He might accidentally drop a word in the wrong ear. Meanin' no harm in the world, Big Bill is about the worst old granny-gossip in the country.

"No, you better do that yourself. You've got an Injun beat both ways from the jack when it comes to keeping your mouth shut." And he could not resist adding, "Look how you've been practicing all winter!"

It was not until after supper that they told the news to the men, warning them to keep it strictly among themselves, not mentioning it even to the KM riders for the present. It was with secret relief that Wylie saw how Steve met the comments and questions. Not one word did he utter against any particular neighbor. His explanation of secrecy was that they were going to line-ride in earnest, now, and try to catch the butchers in the act. By trailing them after a kill, they might be able to spot the entire gang. Time enough then to let the other outfits in on it.

He and Wylie then paired off the riders, planning to keep two out in the hills at all times to watch the stock ranging north and west. And they were not to start any fight. They must not "skyline" themselves, but keep to the gulches. Better, warned Steve, lose a cow any time than a man. What they were after now was information. A dozen men, if they kept their eyes and ears open, ought to be a whole heap wiser in a week or two than they were now.

It so happened, however, that within two days a bitter cold wind driving sporadic snow squalls before it swept down from the north. The riders went out as planned. They found cattle in all the deeper basins, huddled in the shelter of cutbanks. One man got lost in the hills and it took the entire outfit to find him before he froze to death.

It was not, as Wylie pointed out, any weather for butchering beef. The outfit abandoned all pretense of line riding, and stayed under cover waiting for clear weather.

But when the snow squalls ceased and the sun came out, the wind still blew as only a March wind can blow across the northern ranges. What snow was on the ground was soon piled in every gulch and coulee, leaving the hilltops brown and sodden.

The cattle hated snow. They climbed the steep trails to the bare hilltops, and riding the range became an awkward and highly unsatisfactory job. Though new words were coined to express the riders' opinion of Montana weather, the Roman Four gained no information whatever concerning beef butchers.

In Kismet, Steve fared no better. With much care he had worked out a line of approach which should have borne fruit. As a matter of fact it bore fruit with abundance so unstinted that he was really worse off than before.

He asked Big Bill what chance a man would have of selling dressed beef to mining camps and so on, and whether Bill thought the price would make it worth while fattening dry cows for beef. He had quite a few, and it might bring in a little ready cash and save some expense. Buying hay and grain all winter, he added with apparent frankness, had cost money they hadn't counted on spending.

Mention of money always made Big Bill prick up his ears. He was interested at once. He said he thought

Steve had the right idea, and for his part he wouldn't keep any deadheads around him. It was no more than fair, he insisted at some length, that every able-bodied human should earn his or her keep, and if animals couldn't, the sooner they were knocked in the head, the better.

"Only hitch to that," he added dubiously, "is that you never thought of it soon enough. You got a lot of competition, Steve. Most every cow outfit in the country has been killin' off extra cattle and haulin' the beef into town, and peddlin' it around to all the camps. Elk and deer, too—but mostly beef.

"I know the Lightnin' has been haulin' beef all winter, and so has the KM and the Block Diamond, and every other outfit along the river. I buy my beef from Dave, or I'd take one from you right now and pay for it in trade. Glad to. But I been patronizin' Dave ever since he come into the country, and I kinda hate to throw off on a friend; you know how it is, Steve."

"Sure, I know. I wouldn't think of such a thing, Bill. Just forget it. I'll maybe ride around and see if there's any demand for good fat cow meat, before I kill off any. Or," he mused aloud, "if you've got empty barrels enough to make it pay, I might beef two or three of the fattest cows and corn 'em. How's the market for corned beef, Bill?"

Longbow chuckled. "Wish't you'd asked me that last fall, Steve. I could of laid in my winter stock right close to home. You do that next fall, early, and I'll make you a good price on all you want to corn. If it's good," he stipulated with another laugh.

Steve promised to keep that in mind, and strolled

off to the dining-room as unobtrusively as possible. After all that talk and palaver over beef markets, he was no better off than before.

In the bleak days of early spring the detective spirit languished among the riders of the Roman Four. It came to be generally believed among them that some ambitious beef peddler had made one or two raids over back of Cathedral Butte, and lost his nerve before he carried his depredations further. Might even have been Indians, Steve and Wylie agreed. And there they were forced to let the matter rest for the present.

Chapter Seven: TOO BULLHEADED TO QUIT

IT WAS NOT UNTIL SPRING was fairly opened that the problem confronted them again. When it did, it filled their thoughts to the exclusion of everything else. Gradually they had come to believe that they had suffered only from some wandering gang of beef rustlers and that their neighbors were probably all as honest as themselves and knew nothing whatever about their loss.

But while they were riding systematically through the Badlands toward the river, gathering their horses for spring roundup, Wylie found himself staring uneasily into every basin and coulee, now faintly green as new grass pushed up among the old.

For some days he tried to shake off the vague conviction nudging more and more insistently for recognition. When it would no longer be ignored he still was loath to accept the idea, bringing many arguments to bear against it. He even called himself bilious, given to imaginary alarms.

But the foreboding would not be dismissed, and one day after he had taken a longer ride than usual, and taken it alone, he rode into the coulee late for supper, driving no horses before him. Gloomily he pulled the saddle, hung it on its accustomed peg which he himself had whittled and driven into the log wall of the stable, and with his hat pulled down over his eyebrows he walked like a tired man to the cookhouse where the men had just finished eating.

Square shoulders drooped, he ate little, drank two cups of overstrong coffee bitter from long boiling while the cook kept it hot for him. Finally he pushed back his plate and began to roll a cigarette, his lashes shadowing his eyes which stared absently at his fingers.

Abruptly he looked up, swept the browned faces there with a slow glance which came to rest finally upon Steve. "You boys notice anything funny about the range this spring?"

"Yeah," drawled Kirk Latimer, lazily drawing a match along the end of the box upon which he sat. "I noticed first thing the damn range is all standin' on end."

"And yuh never can tell which end's up," Rock Sellers gravely enlarged upon that statement.

Wylie shook his head with impatience. "Quit fooling. What I mean is, there ought to be more cattle running in these hills. Must be a lot more drifted south than we know about—maybe when we rode the hills trying to catch them beef butchers. I've been riding around, making a rough·count, the last few days. There's something wrong, boys; unless they drifted—"

"Drift nothing!" Steve got up and walked over to the window, looking out at the full moon just peering over the ridge. "You know yourself no cattle ever drifted so far we wasn't able to find every hoof and push 'em back where they belonged."

"That's hard to prove till after roundup."

"You and me took a whack at line riding along with the rest of the boys, didn't we? We covered enough country to know pretty well how they moved in every storm. I'm willin' to gamble a new hat there ain't five hundred head—no, nor two hundred head!—rangin' south of the Butte."

"All right, but I'm willing to gamble several new hats that we're shy over five hundred head of cattle right now. Away over five hundred," he repeated for grim emphasis. "We tallied thirty-three hundred and some odd when we turned 'em loose in this coulee, didn't we? If we ain't shy close to a thousand, I don't know a cow from a coyote."

"Can't tell how many we got in these hills, on a range count," Steve argued. "But I sabe cow brutes too well to ever believe they'd quit these breaks till warm weather comes, anyway."

"You've been riding, yourself," Wylie challenged. "Didn't you notice Roman Four cattle kinda scarce in these same breaks, for the number we turned loose last fall?" He tossed his cigarette into his plate and got up restlessly. "If our first herd is going to fade away with the spring snows, there ain't much encouragement to bring up the balance of our stock. We'd be a damn sight better off if we took the back trail this spring with what we've got left."

Steve whirled angrily from the window. "Pull out? *Now?* Quit the best damn range between here and Texas because some measly cow thief is maybe gettin' in his work on us? Nothing doing! If you're right and we're bein' stole blind, I'm here to fight it to a finish." His tone suddenly softened. "And so are you, and you know it."

"Sure, I know it," Wylie flung back. "I'm no quitter, myself. Still, I repeat, we'd be better off to quit now. Only we're too damn bullheaded to do it. But it does rile me to know somebody's got a knife in my back, and not have the least notion who he is. I think, now, that beef butchering last winter was part of the scheme to bust us—figuring it was easy, I reckon, and this one bunch is all we got running under our iron."

Steve returned to the table, dragged a bench away from it with his boot toe, sat down, and leaned forward resting his forearms on his knees. "Tell yuh what we'll have to do first thing," he said. "We've got to gather every hoof we can find and make a count. When that's done we'll know for sure whether we've lost anything besides them that was butchered last winter."

"You'll find we're out several hundred head," Wylie again made grim prediction.

"I ain't so sure. I hold with the boys here. This range is so much of it on end, it's hard to tell without a roundup and a count. One thing—we might get next to something—combin' the hills out, thataway.

"Meantime, we better get word down to Davis right away—Kirk, you can fog over to the stage road with a letter, first thing in the mornin'. You'll ketch the stage goin' south, if you hustle and git onto the trail along about nine, ten o'clock. Winterin' on the Platte," he continued, "they'd oughta be able to start right out. They oughta be here by the end of June, anyway."

"That'd give us about thirty riders." Wylie's tone was a shade less gloomy, but it was even more grim than before.

"Damn right. Thirty riders—and we're likely to need 'em. Scatter that bunch of boys over this country, and a rustler'd have to be smoother than a silk necktie to get away with anything." Steve straightened and looked at Wylie significantly. "I see the Lightnin's doin' a heap of ridin' these days, too. Met old Pike himself, the other side of the Butte, today. Rode right past me. Never said hello, go to hell, or nothin'."

"Yeah, Pike's a surly old cuss." Wylie brushed the ash off his cigarette with a forefinger. "You wouldn't get anything outa him. Well, since we're too bull-headed to quit, the sooner we get the rest of the outfit here the better. If Davis and Moon have done what we told them to, and kept the herds pretty well together, they can start right out.

"And boys," he turned and met each pair of eyes with a straight, hard glance, "so far as I know, not a soul in this country suspects we've got a man or a critter more than we landed here with last fall. Any of you fellows let out anything to the KM, or anybody?"

"Say," Kirk retorted indignantly, "we wasn't hired to go around shootin' off our mouths."

To a man they swore, by this and by that, Kirk was right. Anybody that wanted to know the Roman Four's business could go to headquarters and ask.

Steve grinned and nodded, and Wylie's eyes softened. "All right, I thought so. You're a salty bunch, all of yuh. That's why we picked you fellows to trail the first herd north. Not knowing the country, nor what we might be up against. So let 'er go as she lays. We're here, just a small outfit trying to make a go of it."

"Don't amount to much, but we'll hang and rattle," Rock Sellers helpfully supplied, "and hope for the best."

"That's the idea. If I'm right—and I'd stake my life, almost, I am—and the cattle haven't drifted on south, we'll sure need our full crew before the summer's over. And," he added meaningly, "it won't do a damn bit of harm to have 'em arrive unexpected like."

"Mebby," a man in the shadows observed with a sigh of anticipation, "some fellers around here won't be so damn' paternizin' to us Roman Fours when the boys roll in with the rest of the cattle."

"No," drawled Wylie, "I reckon they won't. Another thing: If we've got to fight, it'll be a fight to the finish; mark that down in your little red books, all of you. Steve, you get that letter ready. Tell Davis and Moon to come a-runnin'."

"Sure." Steve got up again and began to fumble on a high cluttered shelf, looking for writing-material. "By the time they get the letter and get started, the grass'll be up good. They oughta make it through in fine shape. Be about the first on the trail."

"We'll see where we stand," Wylie said in that same quiet tone. "We can throw the cattle all into this coulee and hold 'em here till we make a count and brand the calves. Then—if it's the way I think it is, there's going to be some brisk and interesting happenings around here. I promise you that."

Chapter Eight: CRAZY PUZZLE

FROM THE BUNKHOUSE CLOSE BY, where the men had tactfully drifted (probably assuming that their two bosses might want to talk things over alone), the asthmatic wheezing of a mouth harp with two notes missing could be heard accompanying Rock Sellers's clear but somewhat nasal rendering of a long and mournful ballad beginning: *"I am a Texas Ranger, I'm sure I wish you well-l . . ."* and proceeding inexorably to the tragic verse where, *"We saw the Indians coming, we heard the devils yell-l . . ."*

Judging from the snatches they heard, Rock was doing full justice to the song. There came the rhythmic tap-tapping of booted feet keeping time. Plainly the boys were not expecting to lie awake worrying about the future. That would be showing little confidence in Steve and Wylie, they would say.

Juan, the cook, came in, added more water to the brown beans he had put to soak on the back of the stove, added two sticks of wood to the fire, and went out again to the more cheerful atmosphere of the other cabin. Arms spread wide on the table, tongue thrust out between his teeth, and nose down within six inches of his work, Steve was writing industriously and slowly, with a scratchy pen and deeply creased brow.

"Tell 'em to swing in and cross the Tongue where we did," Wylie suggested, roused from his reverie when the cook went out and slammed the door. "They can't do any better than cross where we did—and they'd do plenty worse if they got hung up at the Tongue on one of those mean mudbanks. They might as well bring the two herds right along together—anyway, close enough so they land here at the same time."

"Yeah, all right. I've done told 'em all that," grunted Steve without looking up from his labor. "I'm settin' down the rowt we took, to the last rock kicked outa the trail by the drag. That suit you?" And he added almost with a groan, "Lord, I wish't they was here now!"

Again the pen went scratch-scratch, like a mouse between walls. Wylie sat absently rubbing the wrinkles in the boot that lay across one knee, and smoked and studied the situation from every possible angle.

If he was right in his estimate—and he was sure he was right, had known it all along, even before he would admit it to himself—if all that big percentage of stock was missing from the range, *who had taken it?* Before they sought redress, or had much hope of protecting themselves from further inroads, they had to know that. Once they knew, they could plan what measures to take.

Of course, there was the Lightning; the dog with the bad name in the country. Wylie did not like the Lightning—as personified by Pike Stoddard—any better than Steve did. Still, the Lightning was a hard brand to alter, and he could not see how it could be made to cover another brand, not even as simple a one as the Roman Four. Furthermore, the Lightning brand was put on the right ribs—the Roman Four branded on the left. It simply did not figure out right, no matter how you worked it.

So far, not a man in the outfit had reported seeing any crooked brandwork on the range—and there were some mighty clever brand readers in the outfit. The hills were full of Lightning cattle, and there wasn't a blotched brand to be seen. At least, Wylie had not seen any, and he had been on the alert for clues. The whole thing was a mystery, the kind a man could go crazy trying to solve. But solve it they must, or—

"Say, Steve, tell Davis or Moon— Which one are you writing to, anyway? Better send it to the one that has the best eyes and can read the fastest, or he won't be through reading that book you're writing in time to start the cattle out. Whichever one it is, tell him we've lost damn near a third of all the cattle we brought up here, and we've only been in this country a little over six months."

"Aw, dry up and let me be. I done told Moon you *say* we been losing cattle right and left."

"All right, have it your way. Wait till roundup, and you'll sing a different tune."

Steve grunted and went on writing. Over a fresh cigarette Wylie Brooks returned to the problem that had haunted his thoughts for days and sleepless nights.

With rustlers in the country, you'd think there would be some sign, a glimpse to be had—yet in all their riding they had seen no horsemen save Lightning men. Not one solitary stranger had he ever met on this range, nor, come to think of it, a cowpuncher from any other outfit than the Lightning.

This seemed to indicate that what few cowmen ranged between the Yellowstone and the Missouri gave

Cathedral Butte a wide berth. Yet all that Roman Four beef had not butchered itself; human hands—hands accustomed to butchering on the range—had done the work.

Why, among all the mutilated hides he and Steve had examined, was there none that bore the Lightning brand? Ranging in those hills were three Lightning cattle to one Roman Four. Not even by accident had one been killed. That, he had to admit to himself, looked like strong evidence against old Pike.

Wylie Brooks knew the cow business and the vagaries of the range as only a man who has spent his life from childhood camping on the trail of the longhorn herds can know it. So did Steve, for that matter, and most of the men who had followed the Roman Four up from the south. And each one of those experienced men, since they discovered the beef butchered in the coulees to the west of the Butte, had scanned with sharp eyes the Lightning stock, looking for the blotched iron-work which is the sign of a cow thief.

But without variation the Lightning brand had been seen to run a zigzag line uncompromisingly from right shoulder to flank, with never the mark of another brand. It was perfectly apparent that Pike Stoddard had been long in the cow business here in these breaks, and had bred and branded as calves all the stock he owned, or all that Wylie had seen. There simply was no mark on Lightning cattle save Stoddard's own brand.

The pen stopped scratching. Steve folded several sheets of closely written paper, licked the flap of the envelope into which the sheets fitted snugly, pounded the flap down with his fist, addressed the letter with large curly capitals, and gave a great sigh over a hated task well done at last. He looked a question at his partner, and Wylie answered it.

"Yeah, I've been getting right down to scratching gravel and leanin' into the collar, whipping my brain into doing some eight-mule pulling to get this damn cattle stealing straightened out in my mind," he said with a wry grin. "I've been doing harder labor than you have, Steve, even if I didn't stick out my tongue as far as you always do when you write."

"Well, yuh still bogged down, or did you get some place?" Steve began to roll a much wanted smoke.

"You can search me. I've about come to the conclusion, though, that either some gang came into the breaks and made a clean sweep, driving our stock outa the country—though there ain't a sign of that—or about a third of our cattle drifted south and we don't know it—or I'm plumb loco."

He gave a short, mirthless laugh and tamped out his cigarette butt. "I'm a chump, I guess, but I simply can't figure it out any closer than those three possibilities, and that's a fact."

"You figured on the Lightnin'?"

Wylie gave an impatient snort. "If you can work a Roman Four over into that Lightning brand of Pike Stoddard's, I wish to thunder you'd show me how it's done," he retorted. "I reckon our cattle hit the trail for home and kept on going, and we failed to wake up to the fact they'd pulled out."

He stood up and stretched his slim body, palms touching the roof. "Just the same," he added stubbornly, "I for one am going to keep right on the mystery till I know what son-of-a-sea-cook butchered our cows. There's no guesswork in that. We know damn well it was done. Wolves don't as a rule carry skinning-knives in their teeth."

"But right now at the present time," Steve made laconic amendment, "you're going to crawl into your blankets and git some sleep. And never mind whether these wolves up here pack skinnin'-knives or not."

"Human wolves excepted," grunted Wylie, and let it go at that.

Chapter Nine: EARLY ROUNDUP

CATHEDRAL BUTTE'S LONG BLACK SHADOW of late afternoon lay with its point far to the east end of the coulee. Its darkest shade covered the deserted cabins and stables and sheds, its corrals lying empty and silent, pole wings yawning wide to the waving grass of the meadow.

Already the wild things had discovered that here was safe and vacant shelter, and had moved in and taken possession of what nook and corner most appealed to them. Two meadow larks were casting proprietary eyes upon the depleted woodpile, hopping from chip to stick to log, discussing the exact center of what might be termed the safety zone it offered.

They had need to exercise much care. Their just completed nest, in which the missus was preparing to snuggle down and lay what she was positive would be the first egg that spring in the coulee, had been trampled flat under Wylie Brooks's sunfishing bronk. The expectant mother had barely escaped with her life, her flailing wings actually fanning the nose of the startled horse. She wanted this new nest set well back under the center of the pile, but her husband suffered from a rat complex and thought dark nooks under logs too dangerous.

A cottontail, dodging out from the other side of the heap they were considering, startled them into flight until they saw it was merely a rabbit, as harmless to their housekeeping arrangements as any creature could be. The rabbit hopped along the path to the cookhouse door and sat on the doorstep looking all around and wrinkling his nose, testing the strange odors of the place before he made himself at home.

In the stable, pack rats were busy. A pair of polecats dug for grubs in the manure pile just outside. Robins walked boldly in the horse corral, and two muskrats disported themselves in the hoof-trampled, deep trail beside the waterhole in the creek.

Bumping, lurching in and out and around the arid yellow outcroppings of sandstone and rubble, chuckling along in green, flat coulee bottoms, the Roman Four mess-wagon pursued its hazardous way wherever it must that hungry riders might be fed.

Juan, the Mexican cook, drove his four-horse team with uncanny skill, following what the pilot riding ahead of him chose to consider a trail; though it was no trail at all but only a line of least resistance to hoofs and wheels, in a network of dry washes, unexpected ridges blocking the way; or sudden depressions with rocks and close-growing willows to bar further prog-

ress. With all these drawbacks, Juan still kept one eye
upon a pan of bread dough that seemed always in imminent danger of running over the edge of the huge
dishpan containing it.

Rattling along behind him, the driver of the bed-
wagon bounced high on the spring seat he rode, and
swore impartially at Juan for his fast driving, at the
mounted pilot for leading them through such impassa-
ble trails, and at the country that was so rough.

Red with his chronic state of anger, braced and
vociferous, he nevertheless kept the mess-wagon in
sight save on the sharpest turns, and usually had at
least two wheels of his own vehicle on the ground
simultaneously. Which, all things considered, was good
driving.

Dave Spellman galloped up from behind, passed the
swearing driver of the bed-wagon by the simple process
of running his horse along the rounded hillside above
the wagon at a level which flung gravel in the outraged
driver's face, passed Juan where the gulch was a little
wider, and pulled his sweating horse down to a trot
beside the surprised pilot.

"Hello, Bill," he greeted with the freedom of an old
acquaintance. "Thought I never would overhaul you
fellows. I heard your outfit was starting roundup already. Brought a man over to ride with you for a
while. He turned his string in with the saddle bunch
back there, and I expect he's busy right now telling
the wrangler what a hell of a country this is."

Bill glanced grinning over his shoulder. "What he'd
oughta do is come on up and listen to Sorry, back
there on the bed-wagon, for a while. He could learn

things, maybe, about all the different ways of cussing out a country."

"Yeah, I heard him as I rode by. Tearing it off in chunks, by the sound. Where's the rest of the boys?"

"Pacin' along ahead a mile or so, I expect." The pilot cast a measuring glance at a low cutbank, estimating according to past experience just how far the wagons could tilt on a sidehill without turning bottomside up. Not that he personally minded so much—he was a youth who craved excitement—except that it invariably disrupted meals for a day at least when the mess-wagon turned over on its back.

Eating came before variety in the young man's category of things to be desired. At the last moment, having taken a second long glance, caution forbade his leading the wagons straight ahead. He therefore swung off to the right, looking for a crossing that offered some hope of avoiding disaster.

"Damn this pilotin'," he observed plaintively to the KM owner as he put his horse across the wash and pulled up on the farther side to wait and see if the wagons made it safely. "Sorry bawls me out for every bump, like as if I made all this hell's brew myself. And Juan, back there, is plumb loco when he gits loaded up and on the move."

"Why, he struck me as being a darn good driver," Spellman said soothingly.

"It ain't his drivin', it's stoppin' every ten rod to punch down that damn bread in the pan. I never yet knowed it to fail. Any time we got to move camp, that damn' greaser's got a batch of bread raisin'. Makes no difference how far we got to go ner when we're s'posed to git there, you can figure Juan's goin' to kill an hour or two punchin' down bread dough."

Juan made the crossing, and the pilot started on. But he was uneasy and kept looking back over his shoulder. "I reckon he's about due to call a halt," he grumbled. "Ain't stopped the parade for 'most an hour. Yup—what'd I tell yuh? Bread punchin' will now go on for Lord knows how long. One good thing," he added more optimistically, "it gives Sorry a chance to ketch up. But that greaser's plumb crazy, I tell yuh. I've made bread m'self. It don't take all the punchin' and proddin' Juan gives it."

"Still, Juan makes wonderful bread," Dave still defended the cook. "I wish we had somebody over at the KM that could hand out the kind of meals your little greaser puts together. Juan certainly has an eye single to the glory of his job."

Bill the pilot merely grunted, his manner implying that while Juan's cooking might be all right, his manner of combining camp-moving and bread-mixing was all wrong.

"I rode by the ranch," Dave observed carelessly—though a more attentive ear than Bill's might have caught an inflection of studied casualness in his tone. "Thought we'd catch you before you started. We don't start roundups quite this early, up north here. . . . Pike Stoddard must have wanted to catch the outfit before you left, too. He was just leaving the corral as we rode up."

"Pike Stoddard?" Bill turned a round-eyed look of inquiry upon the speaker. "Wonder what that old cuss had on his chest." He shook his head. "First time he's ever been on the place since we come. Rode over as fur's the Butte, one day last fall, and when he seen Wylie and found out we was located there he turned around and rode back the way he'd come. Nothin' to bring *him* to the Roman Four. Nothin' good," he added.

Dave Spellman laughed a little. "Well, I didn't ask him what his business was. The Lightning and the KM aren't what you could call real friendly. Anyway, Pike didn't wait. Forked his cayuse and went foggin' up the coulee soon as we hove in sight."

At that moment Juan the cook shouted to the pilot that he would have to stop and punch his bread down again, and Bill pulled up.

"Next time, we'll have to bake the damn bread right here on the move," he predicted with sour emphasis.

Truth to tell, however, he was glad enough of the interruption. Talking about the Lightning had been strictly forbidden among the Roman Four riders, and Bill was a little afraid he had said more than he should.

So he concentrated upon the cook's vagaries and made no objection whatever when Dave Spellman said he guessed he'd ride on and overtake the rest of the boys. His eyes were slightly troubled as he watched Dave out of sight—and it was not because Bill was worrying over the cook.

Chapter Ten: LITTLE TOADS

"WHY, HELLO, OLD TIMER!" Wylie Brooks shouted, turning to look behind him when he heard the thud of hoofbeats coming up. "Are you lost, or just going some place?"

His voice expressed as much relief as welcome. Steve had settled down into one of his moods of morose silence, and nothing more than surly monosyllables had Wylie been able to get out of him all that morning.

"I brought a man over to work this side of the Butte with yuh," Dave explained. "I just happened to be over at Kismet yesterday, and Bill Longbow told me you were going to start out your roundup wagons already. It's a little earlier than any of the rest of us start —I suppose you're used to it down in Texas."

With a sidelong glance at Steve, Wylie only nodded to that and let it pass.

"Where we come from," Steve roused himself to say, "we don't run cattle by the almanac. We go by range conditions. This here is almighty rough country and we don't know it any too well. It's liable to take us longer than it would the KM."

"Well, yes—that's right, too," Spellman conceded without hesitation. "Anyway, I'd like to put a man in with you. I seem to be shy some cattle this spring, and I thought possibly they might have drifted into these breaks—though they never did before, to amount to anything. See any KM's over this way when you gathered your horses?"

"Not a hoof, Dave." Again Wylie glanced at Steve. But that moody man did not choose to follow the opening. Wylie half opened his mouth to speak, then thought better of it.

So the Roman Four was not the only outfit that had missed cattle. The KM, he knew, ran cattle on both sides of the river, though on this side the Spellman stock ranged far to the east of Cathedral Butte and Cottonwood Coulee.

Had he and Dave been riding alone just then, it is likely that Wylie would have told just why they were breaking the conventions by starting their roundup a good two weeks earlier than was customary. As it was, Steve's frowning silence proved an effective check upon confidential talk on the subject of missing cattle.

Dave Spellman broke the short silence that had fallen upon the three. "I met the honorable Pike over by your place as I rode by that way. Has he got a man repping with you, too?"

Wylie laughed. "He sure as the world has. Fellow by the name of Spellman. Ever hear of him, Dave?" He gestured toward a little group of riders slipping down the hill into the shallow basin a couple of furlongs ahead of them.

"Dick, you mean?" Dave Spellman's dark eyebrows came together. He looked slantwise under those brows at Steve, as if he were wondering how the two rivals for Dolly's hand and affections were going to get along together.

"Dick, I mean."

"Well," Dave said after a pause, "Dick being a first cousin of mine, maybe I shouldn't say anything, Wylie." His glance, however, included Steve. "But it wouldn't be square not to tell you that Dick's a trouble-breeder from away back. It'll stand you boys in hand to keep an eye on Dick, I'm sorry to say."

"Trouble-breeder in what way?" Wylie was uncomfortably conscious of an almost imperceptible stiffening of Steve's neck.

"Wel-l, I wouldn't say he's one of these bad actors that's always building himself a scrap over nothing. I don't mean that at all—but he's got a mean temper, flies off the handle when you least expect it—and when he does get mad he says things most men won't stand for. Just lets his tongue go, regardless of a man's feelings."

He pinched out his cigarette, spat on it from force of habit, and tossed it away from him. "He's worked so blame long for Pike Stoddard that he thinks the sun rises and sets and the green grass grows just to accommodate the Lightning outfit," he summed up his opinion of his cousin Dick.

Wylie slid over to one side of the saddle and turned so that he rode facing Dave. "There's one thing I'd like mighty well to know, Dave," he said, answering the other indirectly. "You can tell me, if it so happens you will. What I want to know is, why is the Lightning so damn unpopular around here?

"Pike is a sour, unsociable old cuss, from what little I've seen of him, and his men seem to pattern their dispositions after their boss, from all I know of them. But there's more to it than that. What's wrong with the Lightning, anyway?"

Dave was rolling another cigarette, and he finished it and drew a match sharply along the roughened edge of his saddle fork. "Well," he replied slowly, "I'm not much of a hand at dragging the full pedigree of other cow outfits out into the cold light of the public eye, Brooks. You know that. And personally, I don't know such a hell of a lot about the Lightning. I never had much truck with them, myself, and that's a fact."

Wylie straightened himself in the saddle.

"All right. I'm as wise now as I was before I asked, anyway."

"No, hold on. I was going to say, I keep my side of the river, and away down it on this side in the breaks, and they keep theirs, and that's about the extent of our neighborly relationship. But—well, there's an ugly yarn about old Pike Stoddard and his men that's public history. It's a wonder to me Bill Longbow hasn't told you all about it before this. He's the first one that told me—though I've had it from other sources since, and it's always told the same."

"Never heard a thing but the horrible tale of how old Pike hauls all his supplies in from outside, refusing to patronize home industry," chuckled Wylie. "Bill tell you anything more than that, Steve?"

"Not a thing," Steve came out of his silence long enough to answer.

"Well, of course, you fellows being strangers here, and a—well, not a big outfit as spreads are reckoned up north here, maybe Big Bill—" He hesitated, looking slightly embarrassed.

"Little toads in a big puddle," Steve looked up to assist. "Go on, Spellman. Don't mind us—me and Wylie's used to hopping small and modest."

Dave Spellman colored under his tan. "Fact is, this old story kind of concerns small outfits. A lot smaller than yours. The Roman Four, with a dozen riders, don't stack up so bad among the rest, and you know it. I wasn't meanin' any offense, boys. But, you know— Bill Longbow would likely think maybe this yarn would be kinda ticklish to tell to strangers."

"Strangers that can count all their cattle in one herd. That's all right, Dave." Wylie's tone was bland and slightly amused. "That's all settled, so let's have the story."

Chapter Eleven: AN UGLY YARN

"I can't swear to all this as a fact, remember, but I do know the story's the same, whoever tells it," Dave began with seeming reluctance. "This all happened the year before I came into the country, and it was fresh in everybody's mind—I guess that accounts for about everybody I ran across telling me all about it. Eight years—or maybe nine years ago, it was.

"The Lightning used to range their cattle around Fort Logan. Then they moved down into this country and built a winter camp on Midas River, which is about a hundred miles from here. There wasn't another hoof of cattle on that river, and they had it all pretty much as they wanted it for a year or two."

"Kind of a spread we thought we had, here, when we first turned our herd loose in the coulee," Wylie made dry comment. "Then we woke up out of the dream we had of a cow heaven."

"Pike Stoddard really had a cow heaven for a while. Then a fellow from over on White Sulphur happened through, and camped about twenty miles from the Lightning's headquarters. He saw it was good grass country, and wide open—as you supposed this was, I reckon—and he brought in stock and made himself at home.

"Wasn't long before there was more. Nesters, most

of 'em. Seven or eight men, all told (the way the story goes), each one owning a little bunch of cattle. They commenced to build themselves ranches all up and down the river."

"Well, we ain't nesters—technically speaking," Wylie comforted himself aloud.

"No—no, these fellows didn't have more'n two or three hundred head of cattle apiece," Dave hastily assured him. "But—well, you know what a bunch of nesters like that is like, boys. When they eat beef it's 'slow elk,' and there's never a hide stretched anywhere to dry. If a maverick happens along, it's always the long-lost critter the nester's been huntin' high and low for. His brand goes on it so quick it makes your head swim to watch it." He flung out a hand, dismissing further details.

"Nobody seems to know just what happened over there to start Pike Stoddard on the warpath. Maybe the nesters was stealing him blind, as some say he claimed afterward. Maybe he just wanted more elbow room on Midas River. Anyway, the Lightning served notice on all the nesters on the creek, telling them to gather up their cattle and drift, and do it P.D.Q."

"So far, I can see Pike doing that."

"Yeah, so can I. But the nesters, it seems, was dead-game sports. The only drifting they did was together. Bunched up at one ranch, like cows under a cutbank in a blizzard. All, that is, except one jasper that was so scared he pulled out for the nearest town and told everybody he met that the Lightning outfit had give him just twenty-four hours to get off Midas River, and he'd lose all he had left there before he'd take a chance on going back after it."

"That all?" Wylie's look said that this was a tame ending to such a beginning.

"Not by a long shot, that ain't all. Nobody knows how the rest of the play came up; no one but the men that were in on the deal, and they ain't talking. But a wolf hunter happened to ride up the Midas one day about two weeks after that, and he found that whole entire bunch of nesters decorating a couple of big cottonwoods—two and three on a limb."

"Hung the whole bunch?"

"That's the story, boys. Of course, there's no court *proof,* I reckon, that the Lightning did it, but there had sure been a busy time around that nester's ranch, all right. And you want to bear in mind that the nester in town named his neighbors that had holed up at that ranch, and told why. Every man but one had been shot before they were strung up. That's fighting, if you ask me!"

"But as you say, that's one side of the story," Wylie surprised himself by saying. "Most generally a story has two sides to it. They do back where we come from, anyway."

"That's right, too. This may not be any part of the other side—but right after that old Pike brought his brother (there was two of 'em when the Lightning first went into the cow business), his brother and a cowpuncher into town in a wagon, and him and his riders buried their dead in the town burying-ground and bought headstones for the graves.

"That fall the Lightning quit the Midas River country and located over here. As I said in the start, nobody

can swear this is all gospel truth. But that's the story
that brought up the drag when they trailed in here.
And that's why Pike Stoddard is left strictly alone.
Him and his men. That's one reason why I've got no
time for Dick."

"You mean to say, nobody ever done anything about
all them lynchin's?" Steve roused himself to ask.

"Well, no, there wasn't anything done about it,"
Dave admitted.

"Then it's probably a damn lie. I got no use for the
Lightnin'—but that's too many dead men to a tree, if
you want to know what I think about it. I'd want to
see the proof!"

"Well, I felt that way about it myself for a while.
Proof of what goes on out here in the wilds ain't always easy to get, even now. This was all unorganized
territory then, even more than it is now, and the
United States marshals were too few and too busy to
work up evidence on a case, especially when there
weren't any witnesses. You see what the result would
be.

"A dinky lieutenant did stray out there from the
fort with a detail of cavalry, someone told me. But
they never got to the Midas at all. It seems they ran
onto a bunch of Crow braves that considered themselves on the warpath, and these soldiers forgot all
about the Midas River lynchings, they were so busy
fighting to save their own scalps."

"Well, didn't anybody ever question Pike Stoddard?"

"Sure. The post commander did that, when the
Lightning was burying its dead. Pike claimed his
brother and the cowpuncher was both murdered at

the ranch while the rest of the outfit was off on the range somewhere. His men all stood pat on that story. They got away with it."

"Something rotten somewhere," Steve decided grimly.

"There sure was. And the rottenest thing about the whole deal was that the very next winter—so men that lived in the country then claimed—the Lightning took a half-million-pound beef contract at Fort Buford, and by spring every last solitary hoof belonging to them nesters had vanished off the range. So they began calling Pike Stoddard's bunch the Stranglers. Everybody has kinda fought shy of the Lightning since then."

"Lord! I'd hate to have that kind of a reputation," Wylie commented when the somber story was done. "Makes a man wonder where the Lightning is liable to strike next, don't it?"

"Well, yes, it does," Dave admitted slowly. "Just as well small outfits keep a weather eye out, and ride wide of the Lightning. Of course, it wouldn't be quite so easy to get away with that the second time; just the same, I wouldn't want to get old Pike down on me—unless I had men enough behind me to meet him on his own ground."

"Yeah, you're dead right there, Dave. Neither would I." And Wylie looked sober and sufficiently impressed.

As for Steve, he rode as he had in the past months formed the habit of riding, staring straight ahead between the ears of his horse, paying no attention to conversation not plainly directed to him.

The sun was dipping down toward the skyline

when they halted the wagons and made camp beside a willow-fringed creek. Under his canvas shelter Juan juggled pots and pans with his customary skill, and called loudly on the pilot Bill for wood, water, and such assistance as he needed. The short halt for a hasty noon meal had merely been long enough to bake the bread. The evening meal, as the pilot grumblingly stated, had to start from the grass roots—in other words, with potato-peeling.

But at last the hungry men were fed, Dave Spellman had long ago departed in pursuit of his own affairs, and the two owners of the Roman Four were left to digest at their leisure and in their own way the ominous tale he had told. Steve's morose silence could scarcely deepen for any cause. If that old gossip worried him he gave no tangible sign of it but sulked as usual.

But when the night hawk had ridden away in the dusk behind the tinkling bell of the mare that led the saddle bunch, and the weary men spread their bedrolls and betook themselves to slumber, Wylie Brooks lay long awake, following the train of thought which Dave had unwittingly set in motion, following and finding the going very unpleasant indeed.

But one heartening thought at last laid a soothing finger on his eyelids, pressing them down finally to sleep. Before so very long they would not be just a small outfit ranging too close to Pike Stoddard's chosen domain. Come June, the Roman Four would be a spread to reckon with. Then the Lightning—or whoever might be robbing them of stock—would think twice before they pushed the Roman Four too far.

Chapter Twelve: THE COUNT

FACING EACH OTHER across a thin line of steadily walking longhorns, the two owners of the Roman Four watched with narrowed eyes the cattle streaming along between them. Oblivious of everything else, their concentrated stare noted each animal that filed past. Steve's lips moved constantly as he gazed. Wylie's forefinger ticked like a pendulum moving up and down instead of sidewise.

This was the count toward which all their dawn breakfasting, their hard riding, their bone weariness had converged during the days of gathering cattle. When this tally was completed they would know just where they stood and could pretty well guess what might lie before them.

And whether they knew it or not, the serious import of this afternoon's work was written in their faces. Wylie's features had sharpened; lines that had not shown two months ago were graven deep beside his mouth, that was not so ready now to smile. And as for Steve, his face had a settled look of brooding resentment against the world in general.

Behind them the cowboys held the herd in a compact mass with only one avenue of escape, and through this narrow gap the cattle moved in a steady trickle like sand slowly running through the narrow neck of an hourglass. Methodically, endlessly, unhurriedly, the count went on.

For four full weeks had the Roman Four riders combed the canyons and coulees, climbed the high grassy ridges, forged through concealing brush in the bottomlands along the creeks. Wherever they went, their hoarse yells sent Lightning cattle galloping awkwardly out of the way, or drove startled IV's before them.

Each afternoon on the roundup ground chosen that morning by Wylie or Steve—or both—the gathered cattle were held while any animal not a Roman Four was cut out of the herd. Dick Spellman took charge of the Lightning-branded cattle, hurrying them back out of the way. Bruce Orcutt, riding for Dave Spellman, was patient and watchful; yet when the roundup was over, he took his string of horses and his bedroll and went home with not a single KM animal to show for his four weeks in the saddle.

Day after day the swelling herd of IV's was pushed slowly back toward the home coulee lying under the shadow of Cathedral Butte. Night after night the monotonous crooning of the circling guards lulled cattle and resting cowboys alike. A more thorough roundup never swept that particular section of the Badlands. If a Roman Four critter had been overlooked in those hills, Rock Sellers had declared, it must have crawled into a coyote hole somewhere.

And in all their riding, in spite of the watchfulness of that keen-eyed crew of men, there had not been any sign of "crooked" brand work on any of the Lightning stock. Roman Four and Lightning cattle occupied that section of country exclusively. As has been stated, not a KM animal had been discovered; nor a Block Diamond, for that matter.

Lightning riders they had met nearly every day.

Twice they had been practically compelled, because of the roughness of the country, to throw their day's gathering into one herd and there separate them.

Those herds had been worked in an atmosphere of smoldering hostility. Afterward Pike Stoddard had ridden over and suggested that the Roman Four send a representative to ride with the Lightning roundup, which was moving farther on to the west, up the river.

Kirk Latimer was the man chosen for that diplomatic mission, and just that morning he had returned to Cathedral Butte with a little bunch of fifty-four head.

"The Lightning range has been pretty well cleaned up," he announced to Wylie. "Stoddard told me there might be a few more. He said I had better come on back just to make sure our missin' cattle ain't bein' see-questered back in the basins along the river. That's what he called it, Wylie: see-questered."

"Oh, he did, hunh? And how did old Pike Stoddard find out we've missed some cattle?"

"Well, now, you can search me, Wylie. I shore never let out a word about it. Mebby Dick Spellman might of picked up somethin' about it around camp. That's what Pike said to tell yuh. I don't know any more'n that. Them's his identical words."

"Well, go on back, then. But say, Kirk, you better kinda keep your eyes peeled on your own account. Make damn sure they don't take a notion to sequester *you* in one of those basins he speaks of!" And although he laughed a little when he said it his eyes held no amusement whatever.

"They won't try nothin' like that on me, Wylie, and

I don't give a damn what it means." Kirk started to ride away, then turned back again, as Wylie rode on. Kirk's mouth stretched in a broad grin.

"Say, that reminds me I got a funny story I'll tell yuh sometime, Wylie." He glanced aside at Dick Spellman sitting moodily on his horse not far away. "It'll keep till I get back from the Lightnin', I reckon. But it shore is funny."

With that tantalizing remark and a mysterious wink, he loped away, apparently well pleased with the effect he had created. Wylie had been half tempted to ride after Kirk and demand the story that was so funny and that, if his eyes did not lie, concerned Dick Spellman in some way. There was mystery enough to worry over, in Wylie's opinion, without Kirk adding this new puzzle which would harry Wylie's imagination now like a lone mosquito humming inside a closed tent at night.

But then the boys had pushed the cattle into this small, high-walled basin and strung them out toward the narrow outlet for the count. After that Wylie had no time to wonder what Kirk Latimer had on his mind. The world, so far as he was concerned with it, had narrowed down to this thin trickle of cattle which must be counted to the last yearling as it ambled past him.

As the last cow walked down the trail and joined the grazing herd on the green flat beyond the basin, Wylie slowly counted the pebbles he had dropped into his hat. Each pebble represented a hundred cattle, young and old, bearing the Roman Four brand. There were twenty pebbles, and three careful countings could not stretch that number.

With a gesture of apathetic acceptance he dumped the stones on the ground at his feet, pulled out the makings, and began abstractedly to roll a cigarette, his fingers performing the deft manipulation from force of habit without any help from his mind.

Chapter Thirteen: SPOILING FOR A FIGHT

ROCK SELLERS, who had let his horse doze while the rider kept his gaze glued upon the moving line, reined around and rode slowly over to where Wylie stood with his palms now cupped around the match blaze he was holding to the cigarette between his tightened lips.

"Nobody told me to keep cases on 'em," he said with a diffident concern in his voice. "But I was stationed over here, right where I couldn't hardly help countin' as they went by." He hesitated. "I made it a little over two thousand."

"Thirty-nine over." Wylie painstakingly put out the match flame before he dropped the stub to the ground and set his heel on it.

Sellers stiffened in the saddle, though he could not have been surprised. "Somebody is stealin' us blind," he said with harsh conviction. Though he did not own a hoof of the Roman Four cattle, and though he must have known his wages would be paid regardless of this disaster, he yet identified himself unconsciously as one of the losers.

"Kinda looks that way, don't it, Rock?" Wylie took a long pull at his cigarette. His eyes at that moment held a bleak look. "Quite a shrinkage of beef between fall and spring!" He laughed. "Twelve or thirteen hundred head gone, out of a little over three thousand we turned loose last fall. And it wasn't a bad winter, either. How's that for getting rich off cattle up north here?"

"She's a hard proposition, all right." Rock wound the reins around the saddle horn and got out his own tobacco and papers. "Us boys have all of us had our own suspicions of somethin' under cover in these breaks. We ain't one of us able to lay a finger on a thing. So we ain't been sayin' anything."

"I don't see as there's anything much to say, Rock."

Sellers slid his eyes sidewise in a quick glance. "There is this much to say, Wylie. I don't know as it's goin' to be any news to yuh, but the boys all want you and Steve to bear this in mind: If you get onto who done this, and things come to a showdown or anything like that, there ain't a man in the outfit you can't count on till hell's no bigger'n a bullet ladle. All you got to do, any time, day er night, is say the word. We're right with you and Steve, bigger'n a wolf."

"We know that without being told," Wylie said softly, not looking at the lank cowboy. And without another word Rock pulled his hat lower over his eyes and rode off to join the others.

Wylie mounted his horse and trotted over to where Steve still remained, evidently lost in his own gloomy meditations.

"What did you get, Steve? I made it two thousand and thirty-nine."

Steve looked up from frowning at the toe of his boot

where it thrust through the stirrup. He sent a resentful glance out through the basin's mouth to where the cattle fed in placid unconcern over the worry they were causing these two.

"Two thousand thirty-eight," he answered sourly. "We'll get rich fast, at this rate—I don't think!"

"It's hell, but I knew it a month ago. Far as I can see, there's nothing we can do but take our medicine till we get this thing figured out," Wylie told him. "We'll just have to ride and watch. Somebody's foot is going to slip, sooner or later, Steve. Thieves' luck won't stay with 'em forever. Wait till the rest of our outfit gets here."

"They oughta be here in two, three weeks," Steve said without a change of expression. "I don't see where their comin' is going to change things much—more cattle to be stole, looks like."

"When we get all our men here," Wylie declared, "we can cover the country a heap better than we've been able to do. Some rustler will tip his hand—you wait and see if things don't begin to pop!"

"Let 'em pop! The sooner the better."

"The boys," said Wylie, "are r'arin' to go. Rock gave me a pretty strong hint that the outfit is spoiling for a fight."

"They'll likely git a chance, 'fore we're through here." Steve slid straight in the saddle and looked at Wylie as if he had just remembered something. "That KM man was bellyachin' to me before he pulled out for home."

"Bruce Orcutt, eh? What was on his mind?"

"Well, he told me, kinda like it was to be kept under

our hats, that the KM and the Block Diamond has both been losin' a lot of cattle all winter. He didn't know Dave told us that long ago, I reckon. He says they been doing the same as we done, sayin' nothing and keepin' their eyes peeled. Said he could see we're up against the same proposition, is why he told me."

"Butchering, or cattle vanishing off the range, or both?"

"Both, I reckon. Bruce had one piece of news, though. He says they're talking some of pulling stakes and huntin' a range somewhere else."

"Hunh! That don't sound so good, Steve. What did you tell him?"

"Told him nothin'. What he could see for himself was his own business, and I reckon he drawed his own conclusions. But if he was aimin' to find out something from me, he got left. I ain't trustin' anybody but my own outfit—and none of them better let me catch 'em makin' a crooked move or throwin' in with outsiders. I've got my eye on the whole damn bunch, and don't you forget it!"

Growing suspicious of their own men was something that Wylie dreaded to see Steve do. He was a hard man, once roused; hard and not easily convinced when he had made a mistake. Better lose the whole herd than see the poison of suspicion spread through the Roman Four itself.

"So the other outfits have been hit, too," he commented by way of diverting Steve's thoughts from that dangerous channel. "That means the rustlers have got still less chance to get away with it very long. Everybody in the country will be layin' for 'em. They'll get 'em, too."

"I ain't so sure of that," Steve dissented. "They've got away with it so far, and we've been movin' all hell to get a line on 'em. All our ridin', we don't know a damn thing more'n we did when we started."

"That doesn't mean we never will find out. This kind of thievin' can't go on forever, Steve. You remember how that bunch of buffalo hunters turned cattle thieves when the buffalo commenced to disappear? You remember how they just about broke the Morgan outfit, down on—"

"That's cheerful reminiscence, I must say!" Steve snorted. "Few more years, and folks'll be askin' each other do they remember the time when rustlers broke the Roman Four, up in the Cathedral Butte country! That your idea of lookin' on the bright side of things, Wylie?"

Wylie grinned to himself. At any rate he was pulling Steve out of a dangerous mood. But what he said was: "You remember how those buffalo hunters were caught, and how the Morgans got back most of what they lost? That's what I mean.

"And then there's that time the Twin Thompsons got ambitious and ran their iron on all those Ogalalla cattle, three thousand head in two years. Pretty smooth work. They got away with it for a while. But you know how they wound up.

"That's what I'm trying to point out to you, Steve, that we'll get these rustlers and get them right. They can't pull a wholesale stealing like this and never get caught. Some fine morning we'll see what's probably laying right under our noses now, if we only knew

what it was. Then we'll have these jaspers right where
we want them."

Steve's face twisted into a bitter smile. "And will you
tell me where all this talk is goin' to bring us back
them thousand and more cattle we lost? Look out
there!" He waved a clenched fist toward the grazing
herd. "Robbed of a good big third of what we brought
into the country, and we ain't even been here a year
yet!

"Robbed, or we've lost 'em like a bunch of damn
tenderfeet! That's what I'm interested in right now. I
don't give a damn what outfit was robbed, or how they
found out who done it down south—our job is to find
out what went with them cattle of ours!"

Chapter Fourteen: THE VANISHING HERD

THAT AFTERNOON THE ROMAN FOUR branded calves,
which, because of the rustlers' activities, were far short
of what they should have been. Then, leaving three
men at the ranch, they pulled out early next morning
with their wagons, heading first for Kismet to restock
with grub for another try at the range.

"We've got to make dead sure they didn't drift on
south." Wylie repeated his argument to Steve, his tone
that of a man who clings desperately to a hope so
slender that it is scarcely worthy the name. "What I
still can't see is, if somebody stole our cattle right and
left, where in hell they took 'em to."

"Yeah, I'm about crazy tryin' to figure it out," Steve
admitted. "Cows, calves, steers that'll make prime beef
in the fall, yearlin's—they just took 'em as they come,

looks like to me. Kirk kept his eyes peeled, like we told him, and he ain't seen a thing outa the way over at the Lightnin'. Our stock has plumb vanished. Where to, is the question."

"Did Kirk say anything to you about a funny story he had to tell?"

"No. What story was that?"

"That's what I didn't have time to find out. Dick Spellman was close by, and Kirk looked like it had something to do with Dick. But if it had any bearing on this cattle stealing, you'd think Kirk would have told one of us about it. He didn't have to spit it out where a Lightning man could hear."

"Why didn't you make it a point to get it out of him?" Steve demanded harshly. "Time like this, you can't tell what might have a bearin' on what we want to know."

Wylie looked at his partner. What with Steve's interest in Dolly Longbow and his worry over their losses in cattle, there was no telling what mood his frayed nerves might throw him into. Anger over trifles was no part of Steve's natural disposition. Wylie had fallen into the habit of soothing him like a fretful invalid, and he spoke placatingly now.

"That was just before he pulled out for the Lightning again, Steve. I didn't get a chance to talk to him. The boys were shaping up the herd ready to start the count, and he said it would keep till he got back. I've been wishing, myself, I'd found out what it was Kirk had on his mind, but I guess he thought it would look queer if he held up the count while he had a private confab with me. It might have looked to Dick Spellman," Wylie explained, "as if we were framing something on the Lightning."

"And that might bring 'em out in the open where we could get at 'em," Steve retorted. "Maybe it would of stirred up that snake Dick Spellman, so he'd rattle, anyway."

Wylie glanced back at the wagon coming along behind them with the loud, loose rattle over the bumps which betrayed its emptiness. "Well, I ain't so sure of that. I don't believe Dick Spellman would even rattle before he struck."

To this analysis of his enemy Steve added no comment.

"Say," Wylie said suddenly, "he pulled out right after the count, didn't he, Steve? I was so busy I didn't notice."

"Yeah. Acted like he thought we was through, and I never told him any different. When he rode past me and yelled he was going to cut out his string and go home, I yelled back that he couldn't do it any too soon to suit me—"

"That's asking for trouble, Steve, with a man of his stripe."

"Trouble," Steve declared, "is all I ever expect or want with that low-down skunk. Anyway, he never knew we was aimin' to swing south and to comb all them big benches. I sure never told him we was, and the boys wouldn't say a word, even if they knew. We won't have him spyin' on us no more, anyway."

Wylie nodded. "He certainly isn't much like Dave, and that's a fact. You'd never take them to be any relation to each other."

His thoughts drifted on to the KM's loss of cattle. "I wonder if they've missed any stock on their home range, or whether it's all on this side the river. You hear where it was, Steve?"

"Never heard no details."

"Well, I'm going to try and find out from Dave just how many he's shy this spring; must be a lot, if he's thinking of quitting—which I doubt somehow. You've never been over to Dave's home ranch across the river, have you?"

"No, and that's only the half of it. I don't aim to go over there if I can help it—and I reckon maybe I can."

"Well, the KM is fixed up about as snug as any ranch I've seen in the country. Dave's got a good house over there, and all the trimmings of a home. I'd sure hate like the devil to pull out and leave the spread he's got if I were in his place."

"He's a fool to even talk about pulling out," growled Steve. "We're getting the worst of it, ourselves; but if this little bunch of Roman Fours was every hoof I owned on earth, I wouldn't draw out of the game as long as I had a cow brute left."

"I think myself that's just talk, about the KM quitting their range here. Just a bluff, maybe, to throw the rustlers off their guard."

"Well, when our outfit gets here, I sure aim to get busy. Things'll smoke around here, you can gamble on that. But till Moon and Davis come, about all we can do is hang and rattle." His somber gaze swung to the left, and he lifted his arm to point. "Somebody's kicking up a hell of a dust over there, fogging down to the trail. See it, right over that little ridge? Mebby it's the Lightnin' driving a bunch of stock," he decided, and turned his eyes again to the trail.

"Can't be cattle, moving that fast," Wylie disagreed with him after a brief study of the moving flurry of dust. "That's a bunch of horses, and I'll bet anything on it; horses traveling in a hurry, if you ask me."

Where the trail took a turn around a point of rocks, they found themselves galloping straight toward the telltale dust cloud. And such was their distrust of their neighbors that each man unconsciously laid hand upon his gun, making sure that it was not jammed in the holster and could be drawn at a second's notice.

In those last months suspicion rode always with them, and nothing in that wild stretch of rugged hills and lonely coulees was too trivial to be worthy their careful regard. But at the top of the slope they relaxed and rode on more slowly, their faces betraying their astonishment. There was no mistaking Kirk Latimer and his string of horses.

Chapter Fifteen: A LINK IN THE CHAIN

KIRK SWUNG HIS HORSES EXPERTLY from the trail into the gravel wash thinly clothed with stunted sage, and rode on at a sharp gallop to meet his two bosses.

"Hello." He grinned widely as he came up. "That sure was a quick roundup I was on! Hadn't hardly throwed my string into the Lightning remuda till I had to turn around and cut 'em out again. I guess I'll tarry with the Roman Four awhile—unless the angels call me home, which wouldn't surprise me none if it happened most any minute in this man's country."

Steve and Wylie pulled their horses down to a walk as the tall cowboy swung in beside them. Though their eyes questioned him anxiously, they knew Kirk Latimer too well to try and hurry him into telling what he had in his mind. The dozen saddle horses trotted out of the wash, found that they were not being followed, and stopped on a grassy flat to graze.

Steve waited until his brittle patience gave way. "What's wrong, Kirk?" he snapped with nervous irritability.

Kirk lifted his eyes from the cigarette he was rolling, looked from one to the other, and his grin faded.

"That there's just what I'm burnin' up to know," he said soberly. "That damn Dick Spellman came boiling into the Lightnin' last night. Him and old Pike Stoddard had a heart to heart talk down by one of the corrals. This was away late—ten o'clock or after, it mighta been.

"I was up moseyin' around, just kinda gettin' the layout all located in my mind, when Dick pulled in. That's how I happened to know. Looked to me like old Pike was expectin' him, the way he sifted off down to that corral."

"Couldn't you find out what the powwow was about?" Wylie asked eagerly.

"Well, I sneaked up close as I could, trying to get a line on the conversation. Wind was in the wrong direction, though. I couldn't get close enough to hear much. All I know for sure is that they was talkin' about the Roman Four. Pike was asking a lot of questions of Dick, and Dick seemed to be handing out information of some kind—but what it was I couldn't tell if you was to hang me for it."

"That helps a lot," Wylie observed ironically. "Now we're getting somewhere."

Kirk gave him a quick, reproachful look. "Well, that was the best I could do under the circumstances," he retorted. "If I'd crawled any closer there'd have been a shooting scrap right there, and more'n likely they'd have my hide hangin' on the fence today."

"I know, Kirk. You'd get the lowdown if anybody could," Wylie made amends. "It's just our hellish luck, I reckon. Well, what happened then?"

"Nothin'—then. But this morning old Pike comes to me right after breakfast and tells me there's no use my wasting time there no longer, because they're about through gatherin' cattle, and he don't think there's any more Roman Fours over that way, anyhow. And a few more whys and whereases, all of which meant that he didn't want me hangin' around there no more.

"I come damn near tellin' him so to his face, but I remembered my bringin' up and acted polite as I could. So I cut out my string and bid the Lightnin' a fond farewell. Wouldn't of surprised me much if I'd arrived here packin' more lead than I had in my gun and belt, but nobody said or did a thing out of the way, far as I could see."

"What's the matter with that bunch?" Steve demanded gruffly. "Didn't you get next to anything at all?"

"No, sir, not a damn thing I could put my finger on, and that's what looks scaly to me. So far as I could see, everything is straight as a string at the Lightnin', and all their stock is fairly hollering clean brand and title. And that in itself looks mighty suspicious to an old rannie like me.

"There's something queer about the Lightnin', but what it is I'll swear I don't know. They didn't do nothin' and they didn't say nothin', but you'd think I was comin' down with a bad case of smallpox and they was afraid of catchin' it. And they handled Roman Four cattle like it pained 'em," Kirk snorted.

"What was that funny yarn you said you had to tell me?" Wylie asked, shifting himself in the saddle so that his weight rested all on one stirrup, and reaching out for Kirk's tobacco sack.

"Oh, that? I reckon I didn't tell you about that, did I? That there's the darnedest queerest thing I ever seen," he said musingly. "I been doin' a lotta thinkin' about that, and I still don't sabe the deal.

"Way it happened, awhile back—I hadn't been reppin' with the Lightnin' very long then—we was workin' down below here then, next the river—and I could see that the Lightnin' boys was all swelled up over somethin'. 'Course, I wasn't goin' around asleep none of the time; I come mighty near knowin' every move that was made around camp. So when a couple of the boys hunted up old Pike Stoddard and got him off to one side for a war talk, I begun to prick up my ears right then.

"That's about all I could do," he added dryly. "I wasn't watchin' the Lightnin' a damn bit closer than they was me. Pike, he studies a while, smokin' and lookin' down his nose. Then he picks out four men from the crew, and they throws together a packadero outfit that same afternoon. The horses is run in special and corralled and these four cuts out three apiece—and take my word for it they was rim-riders every one of 'em. I'd watched 'em turnin' cows and I know whereof I speak. So, long about sundown these jaspers pull outa camp, and nobody sayin' a word about where they're goin' or what they expect to do when they git there."

"That all?" Wylie asked impatiently when Kirk fell silent.

"Well, no, it ain't. Not by a long shot. I keeps an ear to the ground, as you might say, 'cause I'm burnin' up to know what it's all about. But nobody explains a thing. And when I takes a chance and says something about how cattle will get into such ungodly places it takes a pack outfit to haze 'em outa there, I gets nothin' but the bad eye from the hull outfit, and any talkin' I want to do, I have to do it to myself from then on.

"Now here's what happened, and your guess is as good as mine: Pike and them four was gone three days, and when they come back again two of the best horses they took with 'em is missin'. The one old Pike hisself rode outa camp comes back with a streak across his hips that I'd take oath was made by a bullet. One of the four men he had with 'im looked about all in, and walked with a stiff leg—what little he walked at all. Pike takes him off to the home ranch, and that's the last I seen of him. He never showed up at the roundup no more." His glance went slowly from one to the other. "That's the tale, and I leave it to you boys if it ain't damn funny!"

They had been walking their horses while they talked. Now the wagon overtook them, slowed to a halt as they pulled out of the trail for it, and when Wylie waved Juan on toward the river he rattled away trailing a thick cloud of gray dust behind him. Half a mile behind them galloped the riders of the Roman Four.

Steve straightened himself in the saddle with something of his old look of decision that Wylie knew so well. "Well," he said, glancing at Kirk Latimer, "seein' you don't know anything, there's nothin' much to be said. You can go on and turn your horses out, and then your time's your own till sunup tomorrow. You can pick us up out on the flat south of the Butte. Can't say just where—you'll know by the dust. We're goin' to cut a wide circle south and see what we can pick up out that way."

"I'll be seein' you, then," Kirk said tersely and spurred out after the string of saddle horses.

Steve and Wylie rode on after the wagon, saying nothing. Another link had been added to the slender chain of circumstance which strengthened their suspicions against the Lightning. They passed Juan and rode down the long ridge that brought them to the river—and also gave them a glimpse of the Lightning ranch, a mile or two above the ford.

Wylie threw away a cigarette stub and turned a troubled face toward his partner. "I'm like Kirk," he said slowly and emphatically. "I'd sure like to *know!*"

"And I," Steve retorted with still more emphasis, "am sure going to know, before I'm through with this game."

Chapter Sixteen: DEEPENING MYSTERY

OVER IN KISMET, Big Bill Longbow was offering to bet anything you liked that the *Golconda,* the boat which supplied him with everything he needed save customers, was stranded on a sandbar somewhere, and wouldn't put her nose around the point below the ford for a week; all of which wheezing preamble was evidently in preparation for a sharp rise in the price of Kentucky whisky, which he humorously prophesied would presently soar out of sight.

One inferred that it would be a matter of simple economy to fill up while the price remained normal. Wylie and Steve, walking in on this harangue, clanked spurs to the bar and set up drinks for those present, chiefly as a matter of policy. Since there were no more than two or three men lounging inside the saloon when they arrived, their hospitality did little toward depleting the stock. Out somewhere in the back yard they could hear Dolly Longbow singing "Annie Laurie," and Steve set down his glass only half emptied and went out through the dining-room. Presently he passed the window on his way to where sheets and pillow slips fresh-hung on the clothesline snapped in the stiff breeze.

Longbow looked across at Wylie and pulled down one corner of his full lips in a quizzical grin. "Steve's a mighty nice boy," he observed in a confidential undertone. "I wouldn't go for my gun if he was to win out." He shook his head.

"Win or lose, I'll sure be glad when things come to

a head so Steve can settle down," Wylie answered dryly. "It sure beats the devil how a girl can throw a man
off his feet. Steve hasn't been himself all winter."

"Too bad. I don't know as anybody can help him
out much, either," old Bill said regretfully. "The cards
just don't seem to fall right for Steve. Mebby you
oughta give him a hint, Brooks. Near as I can tell, that
boy ain't got a ghost of a show. Might save trouble if
somebody told him so."

"It sure wouldn't save me any trouble," Wylie retorted. "Nor Steve, either. He don't take advice from
anybody. I sure wouldn't want to be the one to horn
in on his personal affairs, and I guess I'm as close to
Steve Tilton as anybody on earth." He sent a troubled
glance out through the window. "Who's the winner—
if it's any of my business?"

Bill Longbow wiped off the bar with slow, mechan-
ical rubbing where none was needed. "Well, 'course
this is only my personal opinion," he replied half reluctantly, "but Dick Spellman's out there helpin' Dolly
hang up clothes, and a while back he was turnin' the
wringer for her out on the back porch. My opinion is
that if you was to go out and ask him that same question, he'd likely tell you it was him.

"I wouldn't bet on it, though. Wimmen is so damn
flighty—they don't never know their own minds for
more'n a minute or two at a time. Sometimes it looks
to me like Dolly's worse that way than the average,
and that's goin' some."

"That's about the way I figured, judging by the
fluctuations of the mental barometer out at camp all
winter."

Longbow drew a deep sigh up from his capacious interior. "To the best of my knowledge and belief, it ain't Steve. I reckon he's a mite too steady and quiet. A girl like Dolly wants a man she ain't too sure of, one that's liable to raise hell most any minute."

Wylie gave a short laugh. "Well, she's away off the trail if she thinks Steve's the quiet kind. I don't know of anybody more misleading. Steve's got a quiet way with him, and that's what fools a person. When he does bust loose he generally lifts the lid a foot or two higher than the other fellow. He may be kinda slow about starting, but when he does—the sooner you hit for the brush the better."

Big Bill chuckled. "I kinda wish't he'd showed a little more hell-raisin' qualities around Dolly. It might of done 'im some good. But hell, every man's got to do his courtin' to suit himself. I sure ain't goin' to try and do it for 'im."

"No, nor me." Wylie pushed back his big hat as if he were also pushing away the subject.

Longbow sighed again, and reached behind him for his pipe, which he proceeded to fill. "I hear you've been losing quite a bit of stock, over your way," he launched a never-failing topic of conversation in the range country.

Wylie scowled and shifted his position beside the bar. "Who told you that?" he demanded sharply.

"Well, you know how such things will get around," Big Bill parried soothingly. "I was damn sorry to hear it, but I can't say I was much surprised."

"I suppose Dick Spellman told you." Wylie was still scowling.

"Well, now, I can't say it was Dick in p'ticular. He might of mentioned it—I couldn't say for sure. It was one of Dave's men that stopped by here and told me. We just got to talkin' about some kind of mysterious doin's that's been goin' on here and there the last year or so."

"Mysterious in what way, Bill?"

"What way? Oh—stock disappearin', mostly. The KM's been pretty hard hit, from all I can hear. I guess Dave's been layin' awake nights tryin' to figure it out. Bruce Orcutt and me was talkin' about it, and Bruce just happened to remark to me that the Roman Four's shy a lot of cattle. I'm damn˙sorry to hear it, Wylie— if it's true."

"Oh, it's true enough," Wylie answered bitterly. Now that the thing was known abroad, there was nothing further to be gained in trying to make a secret of it. "We're going to swing south and see if any cattle drifted out of the breaks last winter. It don't seem hardly possible they did, for we sure rode line faithful enough. Those longhorns of ours were pretty thin blooded and they seemed to want to hug close to shelter in the deep coulees."

"Well," Longbow observed, "it's a tough proposition, tryin' to git along and make a livin' these days, no matter what business you go into. Me, I got my own worries to keep me awake nights, like wonderin' whether that damn *Golconda* is goin' to bust down or blow up or some darn thing before she gits here and unloads my supplies. I'm sure glad I ain't got any cattle to worry me, or I'd go plumb crazy. 'Bout how many you lost—if it's a fair question?"

"I can tell you better after we've come back from down south of here."

"You mark my word, you won't find fifty head of strays south of Cathedral Butte, not if you comb the range clear to the Yellowstone," Longbow pessimistically assured him. "Look at the KM. They're out about fifteen hundred head, mebby two thousand, just since last roundup. Dave was kinda hopin', I guess, that they'd drifted off up the river onto the Lightnin' range—yours too, now. He sends Bruce over to ride with your outfit. You know how many KM cattle you found. Not a hoof, accordin' to what Bruce Orcutt told me. And it'll be the same—"

Three men sitting just outside the door got up and sauntered in to the bar. Longbow broke off suddenly and began bantering them again about the imminent rise in the price of Kentucky whisky. They drank, tried to give Bill as good as he sent in repartee, and lounged out again to roost in a row on the edge of the narrow porch. Through the open doorway Wylie could see them gazing down the river, watching for the *Golconda,* two days overdue.

Bill Longbow glanced out at them and lowered his voice. "They're all right," he assured Wylie. "Block Diamond men. The Block Diamond's been losing cattle, too, they tell me. They're talkin' some of pullin' stakes and moving farther down the river, and if the KM don't clear up the mystery before fall, there's some talk of their pullin' out too."

"You'd think," said Wylie, "that they'd want to stay and clean up the gang. If they'd throw in together it looks to me like they could haze the rustlers out into the open. The KM and Block Diamond know this country. We're strangers and there's some excuse for us."

"Well, now the dirty work's goin' on on both sides of the river at once, they don't hardly know what to think or which way to turn." Longbow hesitated. "Well, mebby they've got their suspicions, but that ain't proof."

Chapter Seventeen: GUN TALK

"WHAT DO YOU SUSPECT, THEN?" Wylie leaned over the bar and began absently moving a whisky glass around in linked circles. Though he tried to seem careless and not too serious, he could feel the blood suddenly begin pounding against his temples.

"Well, I dunno as I ought to say anything. They're layin' low and tryin' to git evidence, see. But so long as you folks are losers, too, I guess mebby I can strain a point."

"We'll sure appreciate any information we can get hold of," Wylie encouraged, when Longbow still wavered. "And I can promise you it won't go any farther than Steve, if that's what bothers you."

With visible effort the big man threw off his restraint. "I do a hell of a lot of talkin'," he confessed, "but most generally it don't amount to much or do any great amount of harm when you come to boil it all down. I'd hate to go to work and name names, and then mebby find out later I'd misjudged a man. . . . Did you ever hear, Wylie, that a certain outfit not so fur from here has got a purty hard name?"

The whisky glass moved in smaller circles. "I know of an outfit that isn't overly popular," Wylie conceded in a guarded tone.

"And if you've heard a word about that same outfit losin' any stock, you've heard more than anybody else has in the country." Longbow folded his fat arms on the bar and eyed Wylie intently.

Wylie lifted one hand to pull his hat farther forward, as if unconsciously wanting to shield his face from the other's prying gaze. The movement wiped small beads of perspiration off his forehead. "But— where the hell do all the cattle go to?" he blurted unguardedly. It was the question that for months had been repeating itself monotonously in the brains of the Roman Four men.

"Well, that there's the mystery." Longbow unfolded his arms and stood straight. "When you cowmen solve that mystery I'll look for hell to be a-poppin' around here."

Wylie pushed the empty whisky glass from him and turned away with a long breath of sheer bafflement. How that mystery was to be solved he had not the faintest idea. If two outfits as wise to the ways of this northern range as the KM and Block Diamond must be were helpless to find the answer, what hope had he and Steve or any of the Roman Four boys of solving the problem, even with an added crew of resourceful range riders?

There was the chance, of course, that the thieves would grow overbold. If the Lightning men were the guilty parties, it was possible that the Roman Four, riding cautiously and persistently, might one day catch them in the act. If and when that happened, the outcome would be swift and simple. There were trees in this country with limbs quite as stout as grew along the Midas River.

Steve came in just then, looking in one of his blackest moods. And though he was not a drinking man as a rule, he walked up to the bar and called for whisky straight. So preoccupied was he with his own thoughts that he forgot the conventional invitation to his partner to join him in the drink. As he set down the glass, Dick Spellman came swaggering in.

Wylie's nerves tightened. The hair on the back of his neck prickled a little. Unobtrusively he moved to one side, leaving both men directly in front of him.

Bill Longbow rose with magnificent obtuseness to the occasion. "Come on, Dick, you're just in time!" he boomed jovially. "Steve's got one drink the best of you, but we can fix that up all right. Have a drink of Kentucky's Best on me. As I recollect, courtin's damn dry work!"

"Damn dry for some, maybe." Dick grinned meaningly. "Better double the dose for friend Tilton, here. He looks like he needs it!"

Steve turned slowly to face him. "There's just one thing I hate worse than a long rope and a running-iron," he said pointedly. "That's a long tongue and nothing but wind to wag it."

"Sure hard lines when a man gets to hatin' himself," Dick sneered. "Ten chances to one that makes it unanimous." He looked at Bill Longbow inquiringly. "Ain't it funny?" he appealed to Bill, "I was just thinkin' it was about time the Roman Four commenced to git wise to itself."

"A man couldn't stay long around the Lightnin' range without gettin' wise to a whole lot," Steve retorted.

"And if he don't look out, all that wisdom's liable to strike in and prove fatal," Dick lashed back as he snatched up his glass and flung the full measure of Kentucky's Best straight into Steve Tilton's eyes. At the same moment his other hand dropped to the handle of his six-shooter.

In the usual course of events Steve's time on earth would have been a matter of seconds; would have been, if Dick Spellman had been just a shade less sure of himself. He made the mistake of overlooking Wylie Brooks.

A split second made all the difference in the world. Dick's gun barrel was barely clear of the holster when Wylie fired. The hand dropped lax and at the vicious crack of the forty-five Dick's knees buckled and he went down in a heap on the floor.

Chapter Eighteen: "YOU WIN—THIS TIME."

BLINDED AS HE WAS, Steve reached instinctively for his gun, whipped it out, and fired again and again at the spot where he supposed Spellman to be. By the time the shouts of Bill Longbow and Wylie Brooks had made him realize that Spellman was down, the low-ceilinged room was swirling with the acrid smoke of burning powder. Right hand gripping the gun, with the other Steve wiped his eyes in a vain attempt to free them of the burning liquor.

With a lightness one would never have believed possible to a man of his huge bulk, Bill Longbow was over the bar, landing like an athlete on the balls of his feet.

"Make that damn fool put up his gun!" he shouted to Wylie. "Holy smoke!" he complained more mildly, "I wish you fellows would do your shootin' outside."

He knelt beside the prostrate Dick and examined him carefully, fat fingers moving swiftly over the inert body, coming to rest in the thick mop of brown hair. He looked up, mouth stretched in a sardonic grin.

"By gosh, you can't beat a fool for luck!" he said with a long sigh of relief. "I'll be damned if you didn't just graze the top of his head and knock him out. Creased him, slick as a whistle! I wish't I knowed whether you aimed to do that, or whether it was a case of plain bad shootin'." He eyed Wylie curiously.

"He'll come to in a minute," the young man said calmly, taking the gun from Steve's unresisting hand. "You say you don't want any shooting in here, Longbow. I'd advise you, then, to take Dick's gun and put it out of sight somewhere."

Big Bill got to his feet and stood looking from one to the other. "If I take one gun I'll have to take 'em all," he said, something approaching a snarl in his voice. "You shore had a close call, Steve, and don't you forget it. Biggest wonder in the world that Dick didn't throw a bullet instead of that whisky. Better think twice before you start anything again with this jasper. Can't make nothin' by goin' hell-bent after trouble the way you done just now."

"You brought trouble on the run, yourself," Wylie accused him flatly. "That was a damn poor time to begin joshing, if you ask me."

"He was looking for trouble right from the start," Steve put in, busy with his handkerchief to allay the smarting in his eyes. "He started in on me with his left-handed compliments the minute I stepped out into the yard. We'd of tangled out there if it hadn't been for Dolly."

"That don't make a bit of difference," Big Bill persisted. "Dick Spellman is a damn good man to leave alone; I can tell you that much. Git him mad, and he's *mean!*"

"I don't give a damn how mean he is," Steve retorted. "When anybody starts pawin' up the earth and bellerin' at me I don't aim to back off and hunt a fence to climb. I'll show that whisky-slingin' son-of-a-gun where to head in at, any time he wants to start anything."

"Aw, calm yourself down, Steve!" Bill Longbow stood shaking his head in remonstrance. "I hate to see you git mixed up in a personal fight with a Lightnin' man. The way things are, I swan I dunno how it'll pan out now. I'm afraid you've tipped your hand, and that's a fact. I sure am sorry as hell this had to happen right when it did."

"Well, it ain't your funeral," snapped Steve. "What are you doin' among the mourners? I reckon the Roman Four can just about look after itself when it comes to a showdown."

Dick Spellman opened his eyes, stared dazedly around him and sat up. He reached for his gun, his hand slow and uncertain. The holster was empty. Dick scowled, started to get on his feet, and sat back, one shaking hand going up to feel investigatively along the top of his head.

"Here. Take a drink and you'll feel better. Stop the buzzin' in your head, mebby." Bill Longbow's tone was not particularly sympathetic, but he poured a full glass, which Dick emptied in one long swallow.

Thus fortified, he got unsteadily upon his feet and stood gripping the bar and glowering blackly at the two Roman Four men who watched him.

"Give me my gun, Bill," he growled, adding a blistering epithet for emphasis.

"Why, sure, Dick," Longbow chuckled. He turned the six-shooter deftly in his hands, ejected the cartridges, and presented Dick with the empty gun.

"Oh, give it to him loaded, Bill," Wylie protested with a short, mirthless laugh. "I'll back my partner's shooting qualities any time, against any man in the country. If you ask me, I think this pelican can throw whisky a heap straighter than he could a bullet."

Scowling, Dick pushed the empty weapon into the holster and went weaving across to the door. "You win, this time," he looked back over his shoulder to say. "With old Bill Longbow to stand in with you, you think you've got the world by the tail and a downhill pull! But some day the Lightnin's sure goin' to strike you both—I promise you that!"

"Any time you say'll be fine with us," Steve flung after him. "But don't forget one thing, old timer: There's such a thing as harnessin' the Lightning. One good way I know is with a cottonwood limb and a rawhide rope!"

"Now, Steve, you didn't want to go and say that,"

Big Bill reproved him anxiously. "That only makes matters worse!"

A small thunder of hoofbeats outside checked whatever retort Steve Tilton would have made. The Roman Four riders galloping up from the ford jumped from their horses and crowded in, looking ready for war if that was what the fusillade of shots had portended. The big room looked peaceful enough, with only their two bosses lounging at the bar talking to Bill Longbow. Not even the KM and Block Diamond men were to be seen. The Roman Four riders sniffed gun smoke and looked rather foolish.

"Oh-uh—we just thought we'd tell yuh Juan's pullin' in, ready to load up the wagon," Rock Sellers stammered as they made for the refreshments. "We'd of been here sooner, only we stopped to take a swim in the river."

"That's all right," Wylie answered, as calmly as if nothing whatever had happened. "No hurry, boys. We'll camp at that spring in the coulee about five miles out. Kind of keep an eye on Juan crossing the river with his load, that's all. I wouldn't trust them leaders of his too far. Tell him we'll want an early supper, so he needn't kill all the time there is on the road." He looked at Steve, said "So long" in the general direction of Bill Longbow, and the two went out and got on their horses.

As they turned to ride away the smoke of the *Golconda* bulged blackly above the bank down below the ford. Wylie shouted into the saloon that the boat was coming and Bill had better keep the price down on his whisky, and the two rode away leaving laughter behind them.

"So the Lightning's about to strike the Roman Four!" Steve snorted as they splashed into the ford, their horses walking with heads high, watching the strange sight of smoke rising around the turn. "Well, I reckon the Roman Four will know what to do when the Lightnin' gits there."

Wylie pulled his gaze away from the smoke cloud. "It's funny Dick Spellman would make a crack like that," he said in a puzzled tone. "The Lightning's got everything their own way, as far as I can see. They've got nothing to gain by starting a fight."

"Unless—" Steve hesitated. "Do you mind that yarn Dave told about how they cleaned up that bunch of nesters over on the Midas, and got away with the cattle? They might figure on getting us the same way."

Wylie snorted his unbelief. "They wouldn't have the nerve, Steve! That'd be too rank, with the whole country wise to the reputation they've got. Don't you believe Pike Stoddard's that big a fool. My opinion is that Dick Spellman was just making a big war talk. The Lightning will never start a range war as long as they're left alone."

"Maybe not," Steve doubtfully conceded. "Lord, I wish them long-backed Texicans would show up. I wouldn't give a damn then what the Lightnin' aims to do, or how soon it strikes."

Chapter Nineteen: DEAD END

ONCE MORE THE ROMAN FOUR WAGONS climbed out of the coulee and went bumping away over the bunch-grass range, ruthlessly crushing bright-hued wild flowers under hoof and wheel. Now their way ran fairly level for miles at a stretch, across the benches where buffalo had grazed in vast herds not so many years before. The trails they had made in their mysterious migrations up and down the country in times past still scored deeply the grassland. Juan's supple body bowed to the jolt of the mess-wagon when these trails were encountered, while Sorry on the bed-wagon coined new cusswords as the wagon lurched over the weather-worn ditches.

Farther south the wagon swung this time, so far that rivers and mountain ranges barred the way. The possibility of any stray IV's having drifted beyond these natural barriers was too remote for even the Roman Four's consideration.

Two full days they traveled, stopping only for hasty meals and a few hours of sleep; two days of dogged determination to overtake the orneriest, most homesick cow that ever bore the Roman Four brand on her ribs. On the third morning Steve, usually wagon-boss on roundups, told off his riders in pairs and sent them combing the foothills, looking for stray cattle.

With grim thoroughness they swept the range to the east and the west, gradually working north toward where a broken skyline of pale violet pushed up to a blunted point which was Cathedral Butte. For three weeks the fruitless search went on, and not until the third was there any need of a night-guard. A few old cows with new calves found their journey home interrupted; a dozen or two yearlings not yet wholly abandoning the leadership of their mothers' bovine apron strings. Not a hundred head all together rewarded their painstaking quest. Either the line riding of the past winter had been all but perfect in its efficiency, or the sheltered coulees had proved altogether satisfactory to the longhorn herd.

Disheartening work it was, in a measure. Though it proved an all-important point beyond any possibility of doubt, it also killed their last faint hope that they might have misjudged their neighbors. The missing cattle had not drifted toward the south, that was certain—then where had they gone? As they moved slowly back toward home with their little bunch of truants, that question was ever present in their harassed minds.

Never before had they known of cattle disappearing without leaving some faint trace behind, some clue, however tenuous, that could be followed to the ultimate solution of the disappearance, however mysterious it might be. Usually stolen cattle are left upon the range with brands so disguised that, unless the work is botched, their owners may pass them by a dozen times, read the altered brands, and never suspect that here walks their own missing property.

But the Roman Four riders had almost literally covered every foot of the range where Lightning stock roamed (and the Roman Four cattle with them) without seeing so much as one animal that bore a suspicious mark of the branding-iron. Of that fact every man in the outfit felt absolutely certain.

Now they could add the fact that the thirteen hundred head had indubitably been stolen sometime between fall frosts and early spring, and to that another foregone conclusion that the Lightning brand could neither be worked nor made to cover another brand. Furthermore, it was a brand that could be read farther than any other brand on the range; it stood out as plainly, almost, as the horns; one long zigzag mark extending from the upper shoulder to the flank—no blotching that seared streak.

Cudgel their brains as they would, the Roman Four men could find no way of accounting for the missing cattle. If only the calf crop had been short, they would have understood that very quickly. But with the shortage taking its toll of the entire herd—old and young alike—the Roman Four was completely baffled. As Kirk Latimer put it, they were ready to throw up their hands and admit they were completely whipped for the time being.

In the last big circle to the eastward, far below the range they had covered in the first roundup, Steve and Wylie rode moodily along together, with Kirk Latimer jogging silently a rod or two behind. After this forenoon's ride they were going to swing toward home. For, barring accidents, "Redneck" Davis and Len Moon should be rolling in with the other two herds from the Platte. Just now that prospect filled their minds almost to the exclusion of the work they were just finishing up.

Kirk Latimer spoke what was in the minds of the two riding ahead: "Lord, I'd give a hundred dollars right now to have Len Moon and his bunch here. I bet they'd make the Lightnin' fade out around the mountain without another mutter o' thunder! If the bunch of us together couldn't make that outfit hard to ketch, I'll never turn another cow!"

"Why not wish the whole outfit was here, while you're wishin'?" Wylie turned round in the saddle to ask banteringly. "Redneck Davis is as good a man as Len Moon, any day."

"Oh, shore he is in some ways," Kirk replied, with the freedom of a trusted man who has shared the blankets of his employer times without number and feels himself entitled to the privilege of an argument. "Shore, Davis is all right. He'll fight like hell and never know when he's licked. But you take Len, now —I'd back Len Moon agin any man I know when it comes to nosin' out a blind trail like this one."

He kicked his horse forward to ride alongside Wylie and Steve. "Len's a great old Injun fighter—or used to be. He knows all the tricks of the range, and then some. The devil himself couldn't fool Len long. Why, you know it was Len that called the turn on the Twin Thompsons that time. The hull blame country was out scoutin' around, tryin' to git a line on that job of rustlin'—"

"Yeah," Wylie admitted dryly, "seems as though I remember something of the sort. If I remember right, I was right there in the middle of the ruckus."

"Shore, you was; you and Steve both was there," Kirk assented unabashed. "So you'd ought to know what I'm drivin' at. You know damn well it was Len that smelled out the Twin Thompsons. Then, when he proved it on 'em, old Redneck took his bunch in and fought to a finish before the rest of us got there." Kirk sighed and reined his horse around a patch of brush.

"Yes, Davis is a scrapper from away up the creek."

"But it ain't fightin' we got to worry about, right

now; not till we get the dead immortal cinch on the gang that's cleanin' the range. Point 'em out to us, and I reckon we'll all be right in the middle of the doin's with both feet. But Len's the boy to pick up their trail —I tell yuh those."

"They're both due to roll in any minute," Steve observed; unnecessarily, since there was not a man in the outfit but had watched the southern skyline for the last ten days, hoping to see the gray haze of a trail herd's dust showing above the horizon.

The statement that they were due was so obvious that it went unanswered. Kirk built himself a smoke and passed the tobacco and papers along to Wylie, who followed suit and offered the makings to Steve. Of their own accord the horses slowed almost to a complete halt while their riders cupped palms around their cigarettes and the matches they had lighted. Wylie, half a length in the lead, tightened rein and scanned critically the ground before them.

"Looks like stock has been trailing down this bluff," he said, and pointed to the tracks. He looked at Steve. "Can't see much of a bottom down there—and you wouldn't think they'd trail away down to the river for a drink when that creek we crossed back there has got good grass all around it. But I reckon we better go on down and have a look."

"Sure thing," Steve said grimly. "I've got to the point where I'd follow a cow track right into my own corral, if the critter wasn't in sight that made it."

"And that's no dream," Kirk feelingly attested. "I ketch myself squintin' at brands and studyin' the tracks of our own cattle when I'm day-herdin'!"

They laughed, but their eyes were hard and watchful as they rode single file down the steep bluff, their horses stepping carefully yet sure of their footing as mountain sheep.

Chapter Twenty: A BULLET'S BREEZE

FARTHER DOWN THE HILL the slope flattened a little and the scattered imprints in the sandy soil led them farther to the right than they had expected. Now they could see that the bluff bulged outward, hiding much of its base from sight of the upper level. As they rounded this blunt shoulder they could see far below a grassy, tree-covered bottom sloping gently to the river. From above it looked a sheltered, sunny spot. If cattle once found their way down into this secluded nook they would be likely to linger there content, never thinking of toiling up the hill again to their old range.

"I don't see any stock down there," Kirk Latimer remarked, standing in his stirrups and squinting into the basin. "But there sure as the world has been, all right." His thoughts seemed altogether weaned from his longing for Len Moon. He was eager as a bloodhound on the trail of what might possibly prove to be a clue.

Behind him Steve and Wylie were attentively scanning each small open space of the bottom land, and neither bothered to answer him. Any secluded spot that had not been thoroughly investigated by Roman Four riders might hold the key to the mystery. Things had reached a point where they could not let any basin or valley be taken for granted, though of a truth this looked innocent enough, save for the hoofmarks showing here and there between tufts of grass.

They made their way easily enough down the remainder of the slope and rode directly across the thinly wooded flat to the river. While they still saw the plain imprint of cattle tracks, they failed to glimpse a single animal anywhere. At the river they pulled up, staring curiously about them.

Across the swift-flowing stream the farther shore rose abruptly in deeply eroded sandstone cliffs. Here on the south bank was what, at low water, would be a gravel bar, Just now it told them nothing. Farther to the east, however, a bank of blue sand sloped down to where little waves lapped up and wrinkled the damp edge of it. Here, deeply imprinted in the wet sand, were the jumbled marks of cloven hoofs.

Eyes to the ground, they followed the tracks toward the east, which was down the river. Tracks of all sizes were there, from the dainty, deer-like imprint of spring calves to the larger, deeper impressions left by full-grown cattle. Back in the loose sand just below the last stretch of sod, Wylie pulled up to study the ground. A length in the lead, Steve looked back questioningly.

Wylie crooked a finger, beckoning. "Come take a squint at this, will yuh? Looks to me like a horse track, but the sand's too loose to tell for sure. You wouldn't expect to find horses running down in here, would you, Steve?"

Steve leaned over the horn of his saddle and studied the mark critically. "I reckon it must be a cow track," was his verdict as he straightened again. "There ain't likely to be any horses down here unless it was some old stray—and the Indians keep them pretty well cleaned up."

"Say, we're going to come slap up against a cutbank, first thing we know," Kirk called over to them. "And I don't see how we're ever goin' to get up it, if you ask me. Lizard couldn't climb that steep a bank. Might as well go back, don't yuh reckon?"

Abandoning the blurred track in the sand, the two rode over to where Kirk had pulled up facing a sheer wall of clay and sandstone hidden behind a clump of trees and undergrowth. A good thirty feet high the cliff rose, flush with the water's edge. Obviously, no animal could pass that barrier.

Here, too, the cow tracks became an indistinguishable trampling as if the stock had been moving down the flat until stopped by the cliff, and had milled there in the sand, undecided as to which direction they should take next. Up the bank, beyond the sand, the hard sod told them nothing more than that cattle had passed that way. At the outer edge of the brushy growth twigs and small branches had been broken, but that was all.

Steve, riding back into the open, scanned sharply the bluff, evidently looking for an easy way out of the bottom. To go back and climb the hill where they had come down would be to double back on their own trail, wasting both time and effort.

Suddenly he pointed. "There's three of 'em right now, and I'll bet on it!" he cried disgustedly as three brown objects moved leisurely along the hilltop, heads down to graze.

"Well, they sure didn't make it in one jump," Wylie

made whimsical comment. "They found a trail, and so can we."

"Yeah, I reckon it's a case of climb back up there and take a look at 'em," Steve replied. "We ain't passin' up any critter that wears hair, these days."

Doggedly they rode across the bottom and began the laborious ascent. Before they were halfway up the hill they were obliged to dismount and lead their mounts, stopping frequently, even then, to let the horses puff, and to get their own breath for more climbing. When they had entered the river flat, they had descended some distance above the easier slope. Now they were taking the steep climb below it. This they could see plainly enough from the height they had attained, but it did not make the going any easier to look across at what appeared to be a very passable route into the basin.

It was too late now to go back and take the easier way, and Roman Four nerves were tightening into a state of chronic irritation over small things. Even the horses soured at that labor and refused to climb more than a rod or two without stopping to rest and to gaze longingly over their shoulders at the sun-drenched level below them.

At the top, when the three attained it finally, they found that the little group of animals they had glimpsed was no longer in sight. They would have to hunt them. In silent disgust they wiped the sweat from their faces, mounted their panting horses, and made their way slowly along the crest of the hill. Ten minutes or less and they found the missing animals feeding in a little hollow.

Wylie jerked his horse to an abrupt halt. "By the Lord Harry, they're buffalo!" he snorted in deep chagrin, then gave a boyish whoop and spurred his horse forward, Steve and Kirk at his heels. Buffalo were growing altogether too scarce to be lightly passed by, even at a time like this.

The quarry sighted them and broke into a lumbering gallop which carried them over the rough ground at a surprising rate of speed. Then, running like antelope and pulling steadily away from their pursuers, they swung in a wide circle back toward the river. In that rugged country, and with their horses already winded and leg weary, they knew the chase was hopeless from the start.

Abruptly the buffalo dove into a deep gully that carried them precipitately down to the level below, and went careening across the grassy flat and out of sight beyond a grove of trees. With a common impulse the three disgruntled hunters pulled up and watched them go, in silent acknowledgment of defeat.

"We might have known we couldn't get within a mile of 'em," Wylie grumbled. "We better go back now and hunt up the rest of those cow tracks, and the critters that made 'em. How about it, Steve? I'd take oath those tracks down there in the sand wasn't made by buffalo."

"If they was," Steve retorted glumly, "then we're damn poor cowpunchers. That's all I got to say. We'd better get back down to the river and start in all over again where we left off."

They rode slowly back to the edge of the bluff that bordered the Missouri. In the excitement of the chase

they had lost track of the distance they had come below the river bottom they had been investigating.
When they rode to the brow of the bluff and looked
over, a straight wall of gray rimrock barred their way.
Riding back along the edge, they could look down a
steep, boulder-strewn slope below the rocky wall at the
top. At the foot of the slope lay a thickly wooded valley, smaller than the first one, deeper, enchantingly
green and cool-looking.

"There oughta be a way down in there," Kirk said
hopefully, and dismounted. Stilting along on his high
heels, he walked out upon a jutting point and stood,
tall and lank, on the very edge of the rim.

"You damn fool, that rock's liable to slough off and
take you with it," Steve barked at him in nervous
irritation.

Never had his boss spoken and been so instantly
obeyed by Kirk Latimer. He nearly sprawled head-
long, so quickly did he whirl to retreat. A few seconds
later, the distant crack of a rifle shot came from the
deep valley below.

"Heard it comin'," Kirk gasped, startled out of his
habitual drawl. "Damn bullet buzzed right past my
ear!"

Chapter Twenty-One: NO PICNIC

"Looks like somebody below there ain't very anxious
for callers." Wylie laughed recklessly. "We must have
stirred up something plumb interesting."

"Hornet's nest, judgin' by the sound of what went
past me," Kirk said, glancing over his shoulder as he

lifted a foot to the stirrup. "You go on out there and stand on the edge a minute and listen to 'em hum, why don't yuh?"

"I'd a heap rather be on the business end of the humming, if you ask me," Wylie retorted.

"We've got to get down in there, somehow," Steve declared, ignoring what he must have considered ill-timed banter. "Folks don't take pot shots at strangers without some reason. We better leave the horses up here and scatter along the rimrock till we find a place where we can get down without showin' ourselves too conspicuous on the skyline."

Already he was on the ground, pulling his carbine from its scabbard. Now that a fight seemed in prospect, Steve had come out of his gloom and taken command of the situation as was his custom. Probably because he was a few years older than Wylie, where one man must lead, by tacit agreement Steve was always that man; though not because he was better equipped for leadership than Wylie, for he was not. Yet it never had occurred to either that it was not his exclusive right to command.

"Anchor your horses to a rock, boys. We don't want to take any chance on being left afoot in this country. Mebby we can find a gully that'll take us down in there." And he added in a tone of grim satisfaction, "Thank the Lord they never seen but one man up here. They won't be lookin' for him to come down in after 'em, all by his lonesome."

They tied their horses securely and made their way cautiously out to the rim, walking half-crouched, in the posture of a hunter stalking his game. Once they had separated, even a man on the bluff would have had some difficulty in following their movements, so quickly did they blend their bodies with the gray sage that grew along the rim.

Ten minutes passed in complete silence. Then, off to the right toward the river, a mountain quail called where no quail was likely to be. The stooping figures of Steve and Kirk Latimer converged swiftly upon that spot, and Wylie's eager eyes peered up at them over the black ledge of rock which formed the top of the rim.

"It ain't Christmas by a long ways," he gravely informed them as they came up, "but just the same, Santy Claus is going down the chimney and give somebody a nice surprise. You dawggone reindeer make sure you don't bust a leg." As if the earth had swallowed him, Wylie's face dropped from sight. They heard a faint scraping, the clink of spur rowels on rock, and that was all.

It was a gruesome, black hole into which Steve peered, a splintered gash left by some titanic convulsion of nature, or perhaps a small blowhole through which gases had once escaped, ages ago. But without more than a minute's delay he let himself down into the hole, and as his feet found their first lodgement against the rough sides, Wylie's hollow tones called up to reassure him.

"All right, boys, I'm down."

It was like going down into a crudely dug well, rather small as wells go and neither round nor square. A man might break his neck, but if he took his time and made sure of his footing he had a very good chance of making the descent without broken bones or abrasions.

Thirty feet down, dim daylight met them. Another twenty, and their feet struck the gravel of the bottom. Wylie stood there waiting, calmly smoking a cigarette which he pinched out as soon as they appeared.

"Here's where we take a chance," he announced cheerfully as Steve and Kirk Latimer stood beside him. "Before you go any farther I might as well tell you she's bald as an egg for a good fifty yards from here on down the bluff. You've got your choice. You can walk out and take a chance, or get down on your belly and crawl—and maybe make yourself just as good a target. Me, I'm going to make a run for it."

"Same here," Kirk said shortly, and drew his gun from its holster, looking it over critically before he eased it back again. "Mebby I better go first. My legs is longest, and aimin' at me'd be like tryin' to hit a willer branch wavin' in the wind."

"No use to go beggin' for bullets," Steve vetoed that suggestion. "Take it easy. They're watchin' the rim up above us. We can slip along close to the rocks and maybe git to cover before they spot us."

They had made two-thirds of the distance when a bullet zipped close over the head of Wylie Brooks, last in line and nearest the base of the rim where Kirk had shown himself. An interval of serene silence, and then the report.

"*Down,* you damn' idiot!" snapped Steve, freezing to absolute immobility. "They've got yuh spotted."

But already Wylie had rolled to safety behind a boulder jutting out solidly from the slope directly below him.

"Yuh hurt?" From where he lay half concealed behind a tuft of rabbit brush Kirk craned his long neck to see what had happened. "Can't yuh see anybody, Steve? How'd it be to toss a shot down that way for luck?"

"Slide down here, Kirk," Wylie urged him, sitting up and anxiously inspecting his carbine. "From here down there's cover all the way to the bottom. We can get in the brush down there and smoke 'em up right."

Steve made his way cautiously over to the boulder, and presently they were joined by Kirk. "The thing to do is get a good look at them if we can," he said. "This long-distance fightin' is all right in its place, but it ain't liable to get us anywhere. Come on—and keep down outa sight!"

Another shot spatted against the rimrock above them, evidently fired chiefly for the moral effect. It went high and a good ten yards wide of their boulder. They went on, crouching low, slipping between high sage bushes, wary of all open spaces.

Then, halfway to the valley's floor, Wylie peered cautiously over a boulder, stared hard for a moment, and stood up with a snort of disgust.

"There they go, hell-awhooping up the flat! Four of 'em, on horses. Look there, Steve! See 'em, dodging into the brush right down there next the river?"

They rose and looked where he was pointing. Kirk thrust his long neck forward, his eyes yellow and fixed in a stare like an eagle.

"Injuns, b'gawd! Lookit that red blanket floppin' in the wind! And there goes another one. Well—I'm—

ee-ternally *damned!*"

All Indians roaming that country were at peace with their white brothers, ostentatiously so, one might almost say. Beggars for tobacco, tea, white bread—always ready for a horse race or a trade—certainly not in the habit of shooting white men at sight of them.

"Now, what d'you reckon struck them bucks to shoot and run, like that?" Steve was still staring bewilderedly at the place where the fleeing quartet had disappeared. "If they was out for our scalps, they'd of stuck and shot it out with us. They're four to our three."

"Well, we might as well go on and see what they've been up to." Wylie went climbing down over the huge rocks covering the last slope. "They weren't off down in here on any picnic, I can tell yuh that."

Chapter Twenty-Two: STILL IN THE DARK

DOWN IN THE FLAT-BOTTOMED BASIN Wylie stopped abruptly and stood with head tilted backward, staring up at the bold bluff topped with its brown wall of rock. As his gaze swept round the crude semicircle he whistled softly to himself.

"Will you tell me something I don't know, Steve?" He looked at his partner queerly. "How the devil did them bucks get down into this bottom with horses?"

"Prob'ly," Kirk forestalled his boss, "they got in same way they're goin' out." He turned and made off up the flat, his long, loping stride carrying him quickly out of sight among the trees.

"The damn fool never stops to think them four

might not be all of 'em," Steve grumbled. "He'd go broilin' right into a mess of 'em and think nothin' of it."

But a man of Kirk Latimer's type could not live for forty years in the West of that time without taking risks with his eyes open. Nonchalantly as the tall cowpuncher loped through groves and across the open stretches his darting glance touched and made note of every object within range of his vision. The valley so far was empty and silent.

"Say!" Wylie panted, trotting alongside Steve, "do you reckon there's any chance of their swinging around back and running our horses off?"

"That's a chance we've got to take. Far as I can see, they was headed off in the other direction. It ain't likely they'll come back around this far. They'll keep on goin', if I know Injuns."

Wylie slowed to a walk, mopping his face as he stared uneasily up at the stark, forbidding ledge that walled them in. "If I know Injuns," he made belated retort, "they'd rather steal a horse than eat stewed dog, any day. D'you reckon they think we come into this country afoot?"

"Mebby, tomorra or next day, they might begin to kinda wonder how we got here," Steve said slightingly. "Don't go and overestimate an Injun's thinkin' powers."

"Like I have been yours, if you think for a minute they're going to pass up any bets."

They came up with Kirk Latimer and stopped beside him. Kirk was standing behind a screen of brush, staring across a deep, water-worn gully which seemed

to divide the flat into two unequal parts. Across the
gully was open meadow for a hundred yards or so.
Beyond that, a grove of young cottonwoods stood deep
in undergrowth.

"Right about over there in that brush is where they
was," Kirk told them in an undertone without moving
his eyes from the spot. "I don't hardly think there's
anybody there now, but we might as well wait a minute and make shore."

A cottontail rabbit hopped out from beneath a bush,
stood up on his hind feet and looked around, front
paws dangling. Satisfied, he dropped back on all fours
and went to investigate a tuft of broad-leaved herb
near by.

"I ain't worried if he ain't," Kirk observed laconical-
ly, and legged it down into the gully and up the other
side, Steve and Wylie close behind his heels.

As they trotted across the open space the rabbit vanished with a bobbing white fluff scudding for shelter.
A magpie fluttered out of a sapling top as they passed,
and went scolding away up the flat, proof enough that
they were the only disturbers of that peaceful valley.
They pushed their way through the grove and emerged
into another open glade.

"Nothin' here," Kirk declared in his natural tone of
voice. "I reckon them four was all of the bunch."

They waited, however, drawing long breaths into
their heaving chests while they listened for all those
hushed little wood notes which were their best as-
surance of unbroken solitude. The shrill chatter of
magpies threaded the silence with high shrewish notes
farther ahead. A mourning dove called plaintively

from a thicket down near the river. Somewhere a squirrel chipped querulous remonstrance against some familiar offense.

Then came another sound which brought the three to instant attention, their eyes meeting in swift glances of understanding. A cow had lowed deeply, not far away; immediately afterward a calf had blatted in reply. Without a word the Roman Four men worked their way cautiously around the edge of the clearing toward the sound.

Other betraying sounds came to them as they advanced toward the bluff, cattle sounds there was no mistaking. And finally, deep-set within a larger grove from which the underbrush had been carefully cleared and piled cunningly to form what looked like a natural screen of dead wood, they stood hidden from view yet plainly seeing the stout pole corral with wide, far-reaching wings of living trees, brush, and wire.

A businesslike, competently built corral it was. Big enough to hold a couple of hundred head of cattle with a little crowding, so well concealed that even from the valley's rim it could not be seen in that thicket of tall cottonwoods. In the grove there were no cattle trails at all, but the ground within the wings was trampled like the corral. Inside, fifty or sixty cattle—cows, calves, yearlings, steers of all ages—moved restlessly about, switching their tails industriously and tossing their heads, annoyed by the swarms of gnats that wove their endless patterns in the windless air.

For some minutes the three stood silently surveying the scene, waiting for some sign of human life near by. By all the laws of range logic there should be men there somewhere on guard. For even the boldest thieves were not likely to leave a bunch of stolen cattle corralled like this for the owners to find and perhaps set a trap into which rustlers might ride—to meet a hail of lead from the bushes. That had happened in the past; thieves took fewer chances now.

But the magpies chattered away, busy with their own gossip in the bushes beyond the corral, hushing only when a pair flew close over the three watchers and with startled cries warned the rest. Silence fell on the grove, save when beating wings bore the alarmed birds away.

Wylie moved slowly out into the open and stood, rifle in hand, watching the opposite thicket. Nothing moved but the cattle.

"All right, I reckon," he said over his shoulder. "The four we saw must have been the whole bunch." He walked boldly up to the fence, Steve and Kirk following. The cattle wheeled toward them, then backed and stared curiously, as wild cattle do when they see men afoot. The three edged cautiously up and stood peering through between the rails.

"Just as I thought," Steve muttered savagely. "Every damn one of 'em IV's."

"Them wasn't Injuns we saw takin' off up the valley," Kirk declared. "I'm willin' to take my oath that I've slep' under the same tent and et at the same table with them buckaroos. I thought all the time they looked familiar, just the way they set on their horses. I know it now fer a fact. If that hind one wasn't Dick Spellman, I never seen him b'fore in my life."

With no definite object in view, but acting merely

upon a stockman's impulse, they climbed the fence and went in among the cattle, looking them over for altered brands. Roman Fours, every hoof; big beef steers, cows with young calves nosing at their flanks, younger stock—gathered just as they were found grazing in some out-of-the-way coulee—with not a strange iron-mark on any one of them to give a clue to the thieves. Clean Roman Fours, except that the spring calves were not branded. Here, at least, was one bunch the Roman Four riders had overlooked on roundup.

That other stock had been corralled here the hard-packed soil gave proof, as did the trampled approach through the wings and the trails leading from the place; leading down into a gravel wash which formed a natural chute to the wings, as they presently discovered.

One thing was certain: they had stumbled upon the place where the rustlers had been systematically corralling—and probably re-branding—the IV cattle. But what became of the cattle after the brand had been altered? It would take weeks for the fresh burns to scab off and then hair over properly. Until that was complete the cattle must be hidden away somewhere, and they certainly were not held for long in this valley. Here were sixty at most. Where were the thousand? Had they all passed through this same corral? Probably.

"What I want to know," Wylie broke abruptly from their silence, "is how the devil they got the cattle down here. That rimrock comes down to the river, above and below."

"What we better do is go up along the river, the

way those jaspers went foggin' outa here," Steve said. "If there wasn't some way out at that end, why in hell would they go that way? I reckon Kirk's right; them wasn't Injuns."

"Pretty warm day to be sporting blankets down in here," Wylie remembered then. "I thought there was something off-color with the picture of them gazabos loping off up the valley with blankets on, and me sweating like a horse. I couldn't just figure it out at the time. It was the blankets."

"Tryin' to make us think they was Injuns," Kirk drawled. "You hit it, first crack. Must of used their saddle blankets, I reckon."

"And that," Wylie followed the thought to its conclusion, "shows that they're the fellows we're after, and they had to throw us off the track the quickest and easiest way they could. Plain as the nose on your face!"

"It was the Lightnin'," Kirk repeated his belief. "I'd bet anything yuh like on that."

"One of us better git back up the bluff and look after the horses," Steve decided. "Kirk, I guess you better go. You got long legs for climbin' back up that chimney of rock. We'll see where the outlet of this bottom is, and then we'll be along. You can signal if yuh see any sign, up there."

With a longing glance down the gravel wash they were following, Kirk reluctantly climbed the bank and went striding off toward the bluff, making no attempt now to conceal his movements. The valley was empty of rustlers, of that they were certain.

The cattle they were compelled to leave in the corral for the present—at least until they found the way out, and had their horses under them once more. They plodded on down the gully, too bone-weary to feel any sense of elation over their discovery, though this was the moment they had sought since early March. They had found a few of their cattle, it was true; they had even found the hidden corral used by the thieves. But they were still completely in the dark as to their identity, and Wylie, at least, walked gloomily under a sense of failure.

Chapter Twenty-Three: A CLUE AT LAST

A WINDING COURSE IT WAS they followed, though the general direction held to the westward. And when at last the gravel-washed gully opened its mouth upon the river's sandy, sloping bank, they walked out to face the blank wall of a cutbank much too high for climbing.

Wylie, who was in the lead, stopped short and studied the bank critically. "Shall we tackle it, Steve?" he asked. "I think maybe I could shinny up there, if you'd give me a boost to start with."

"And what's the use?" Steve retorted. "They sure never boosted any cattle up or down it."

Yet the tracks led straight from that bank to the mouth of the gully—though it was true that the loose gravel and deep, sliding sand of the river bank defied any definite tracking at that point. But there was fresh cattle sign, plenty of it all along.

"No, the cattle never got over this bank," Wylie admitted glumly. "It sure beats hell—unless they took to the river. And that don't look feasible, either. But I betcha one thing, Steve: I betcha this right here is the same identical bank we ran into, back in that other flat. Same formation, and no break in it anywhere."

He turned back and walked slowly along the bank, studying it closely as he went. There was no cleft such as one so frequently found in the rock formation of the badlands, no pass whatever. And farther inland the wall heightened to meet the contour of the bluff which it joined.

He retraced his steps to the water's edge and stood there, thumbs hooked inside his chap belt, frowning out across the river. Suddenly he stooped and picked up a stone and threw it out to fall a few yards from shore. At the splash, Steve, sitting on the bank rolling a cigarette, looked up quickly.

"D'you know what I believe?" Wylie asked, turning toward him. "I believe they took to the water and went around this damn bank. You remember that other bottom, above here, had stock trails running down into it. We rode down the bluff, easy enough."

"Yeah, I know we did." Steve drew a match meditatively along the sole of his high-heel boot. "We've got to figure out some way to get our stock outa this bottom and into camp. One of us'll have to tackle the river, I reckon. I'm willin', myself."

But Wylie was already throwing off his clothes. "You keep that gun of yours handy while I go," he said. "May not be anyone keeping cases up above here, and then again, there might." He grinned a little. "You can write your name in bullets on the head of a pin, and all that—but how are you at shooting around corners?"

"Me? Right behind yuh, old timer." Steve lifted a boot to his knee and started to pull.

"Nothing doing! You stay right where you're at. My gun-hand ain't sprained. I was joshing and you know it."

"Mean to pack your gun like a dog does a bone, I reckon, and shoot with your teeth!"

"Might. You wait and find out." He stepped into the water, shivered involuntarily and drew back his foot. "She's sùre cold," he remarked. "I won't be long."

Gun in hand, he waded in, clothed only in his hat. By the time he disappeared around the nose of the high cutbank Steve had his own boots off, preparing to follow if he heard an untoward sound.

He heard nothing until Wylie came splashing back, still dry above his middle, a grotesque figure with his white body, his face tanned brown as an Indian, his hat, and his gun. He was still shivering.

"It ain't more than ten rod around to the next flat," he said disgustedly, "and it wouldn't swim a chickadee. Pretty damn swift, though—but good hard bottom all the way. It's a cinch, Steve!"

His eyes, as he left the river and began pulling on his clothes, held the fighting gleam. "That's where them so-called Indians got to," he went on. "Tracks are plain where they left the water. Same bank we bumped into." He jerked his head toward the cutbank, and then ducked into his shirt. "You know that strip of blue sand?" His voice came. muffled.

"You don't have to draw no diagram," Steve snubbed him. "I sabe the hull play. That bottom above here is lousy with cattle tracks. Good feed, plenty water, plenty shelter—we could (and some of the boys prob'ly did) work that bottom and git a few head of cattle, mebby, and nobody'd think a word about it. All clean as a whistle. Open and aboveboard. And right down around the turn, here, is their first hide-out."

"That's the system, all right." Wylie stepped into his chaps, wriggled his slim body to adjust them, buckled the belt, and pointed. "And across the river there is such hellish rough country nobody from the KM or the Block Diamond would ever get close enough to the bank to look over here and see anything funny goin' on."

Steve stared glumly across to the opposite shore. "Yeah, I've been takin' notice of that, too. Don't look any too promisin' for crossin' cattle."

Wylie was buckling on his cartridge belt, pushing his gun into its holster. "So where the blue blazes do they take the cattle from here?" he demanded with a shade of desperation in his voice. "They don't aim to hold stock here long. You notice there's no grazing signs, and the grass is good, too."

"Your guess," said Steve, "is as good as mine. What do you think?"

Wylie resettled his hat and, fully clothed again, seemed to feel entitled to a smoke. "Well, my guess is that they run a bunch in here and corral 'em, and wait over till it's coming dark again before they go on." His eyebrows drew together thoughtfully as he sifted tobacco into the tiny paper trough in his fingers.

"Yeah. On—*where?*"

"That," Wylie glanced up to say, "is your guess, Steve. I've about guessed my limit."

Steve swung about and scanned the bluff down which they had climbed so precariously. "They sure as hell can't wade around that one," he muttered, "and hit another bottom down around the turn. You can't play that kinda luck twice hand-runnin'."

"Why don't we have Kirk bring the horses on around here?" Wylie decided without preface. "There he goes, just climbin' that bald stretch where we was shot at. *Hi, Kirk!*"

From below, his voice rose clearly to the rimrock. The tiny figure of the man up there stopped, turned, and swung his hat in a long-armed arc.

Through cupped hands Wylie megaphoned, "Bring —the *horses!*" Wide gestures in a modified adaptation of Indian sign-talk made his meaning sufficiently clear, even at that distance. After more shouting, more waving of arms, a faint, almost ethereal *"A-a-ll r-i-g-h-t"* drifted down to them, and Kirk moved to one side, waved both arms again, pointed to the west, and vanished from sight.

Whereupon both young men partially disrobed again, and burdened with clothing and guns waded back around the point to wait for Kirk in the upper valley.

"Whoever's doing it, they're pretty damn slick, all right," Wylie commented, when they were once more clothed and hitting a leisurely pace up the bottom land toward the more easily negotiated slope of the encircling hill. "We'd never of got next to this in a thousand years, only for them buffalo."

"If them damn fools had kept their heads level, and hadn't started bouncin' bullets up onto the rim, we wouldn't have got wise to it even then," Steve amended the statement. "Only, uh course the cattle might of started bawlin' at the right minute and tipped us off."

"We're away down river from where we'd be expected, even so. Wonder where they picked up them cattle in the corral," Wylie went on. "Must have found 'em back here on the KM range. It's a wonder they didn't run into some of the KM cowboys—but I reckon, though, they're all over across the river on round-up, about now."

"Purty slick of the Lightnin', runnin' our cattle down river instead of up it," was Steve's opinion. "Well, there comes Kirk with the horses. We'll make short work of gettin' them IV's up outa here and headed for camp where they belong!"

Chapter Twenty-Four: UNANSWERED QUESTIONS

SHORT WORK IT WAS. To drive the cattle into the water and around the cutbank, across the flat and up the bluff, across the ridges and on to camp was comparatively simple and no slower than such work usually is when the cattle are strong and not too tired to travel. Supper was over, and the faces of the men showed distinct relief when the three rode their weary horses into camp at a walk.

Blankets were warmed with their hard-muscled bodies late that night. To have found a few stolen cattle was like the warm scent of fat deer to a wolf pack. Though the hunting call was chiefly given in harsh mutters, it was savage enough to have held the Lightning sleepless, could they have heard. After so long a siege of mystery and blind guessing, here was a clue at last—and not a man in the outfit but told himself the end was in sight.

That night a pack outfit was made ready and five men carefully chosen for their shrewdness on the trail, their marksmanship, cool courage, and endurance. Just as carefully their mounts were selected. Before dawn the five rode out of camp envied by all the rest, to make a systematic search of the countless small bottoms down the river. Wiry, indefatigable Kirk Latimer rode with them to direct the quest. They carried supplies for a week.

The Roman Four breathed easier after that. The mystery, they told one another, was just as good as solved. What they needed now was proof—a chance to catch the Lightning in the act. After that, the KM and the Block Diamond would be invited to a necktie party, and the country could settle down to raising cattle in peace and quiet.

Unhurriedly the wagons worked their way back to Cathedral Butte, driving before them what stock had been gleaned on these high benches. Four days saw them through with the job, and they turned cattle and horses loose in the home pastures and waited for news from the scouts down river. Upon the report of Kirk Latimer and his men depended the next movement of the IV, and in the meantime the men loafed in the shade and speculated upon the outcome, watched for the trail herd now due, and slept like cats in the sun.

Then the five rode wearily into the home coulee one evening and were met at the corral by the entire crew, including the cook, who left his bread to scorch in the oven if it must while he got the news fresh and first-hand. And the report was worth less than a burned loaf to the Roman Four.

"Beats hell four ways," Kirk Latimer drawled bitterly, and loosened the latigo with savage yanks. "We done combed every bottom for forty mile down river, boys. Some we went into on foot, it was so dang rough. Rock, here, would a drownded tryin' to wade around a point, only we had a lariat on 'im an' drug 'im back agin the current limp as a dead mus'rat—"

"What about that corral, you chump?" Steve broke in harshly. "Why didn't yuh watch that corral?"

Kirk straightened and glanced sidewise under his hatbrim, meeting the shine of eyeballs in the starlight which showed Rock gazing at him eloquently. "That c'rel," he said dryly, "wasn't left alone a minute skurcely. I had a couple of the boys belly down in the brush every damn night in the world since we left roundup. Fact, I was one, most nights. I know the Lightnin' an' I know their voices.

"The cloudy nights we been havin', somebody laid in wait as close to that c'rel as wouldn't scare a cow. Couldn't beat them nights fer rustlin', you-all know that. They never made a move."

It was evident that the thieves had been frightened off by the encounter a week ago, and had not since ventured into that valley. They must have other corrals hidden away in widely separated sections. That was a foregone conclusion, the Roman Four losses being far too great for that one outlet. But it was a disappointment, nevertheless, to have nothing to show for a week's intensive searching.

Over their belated supper the party supplied details. They had seen a few head of Lightning stock in some of the lower bottoms: big four- and five-year-old steers wild as antelope, cows with no calves by their side—strays that had summered and wintered along the breaks next the river. They had also read the KM brand on a few cattle, and some brands strange to this northern range. Twice they had glimpsed Indians riding swiftly across distant ridges. They had jumped a few scattered remnants of the great buffalo herds now gone forever. But of IV stock not a hoof was to be found.

Thus the Roman Four found themselves, after a week of high hopes, exactly where they had been a month before. Unpalatable as it was they had to face that fact. There was nothing they could do save grind their teeth and line-ride their depleted herd with greater care than before, and watch for some clue carelessly left by thieves who seemed almost as unreal as the phantoms of a bad dream. And they must wait with what patience they could for the coming of Len Moon and Redneck Davis with the trail herds from the Platte.

With Steve fallen again into his morose silence from which he emerged only when something especially irritated him, the full burden of responsibility for the morale of the men rested upon Wylie Brooks. Whether Steve had definitely given up all hope of winning Dolly Longbow—whether he still wanted to win her—Wylie could only conjecture. He scarcely believed his surly partner wanted the girl now, after that scene in Kismet. Steve wasn't a fool, and he would not be made a fool of by Dolly Longbow or any other girl. Wylie banked on that.

No, it was the blank wall they were facing when they should be at hand grips with the rustlers. That was what worried Steve and made him hard to live with. That, and the suspense of waiting, with no word from the trail herds. Many disastrous things could have happened between the Missouri and the Platte. Wylie preferred not to enumerate them, and he hoped Steve was too engrossed with the rustling riddle to think of them.

He took to watching Steve more closely, trying to guess what thoughts were shuttling back and forth through the man's mind. Sometimes when they were alone together he would talk of the rustling, trying to draw Steve out of his brooding silence: If the Lightning was doing wholesale rustling, where had they hidden the cattle? On the other hand, if the Lightning's skirts were clear, why should they be immune when the ranges on either hand were being plundered? Fat steers ranged down the river, and they bore the Lightning brand. Why were they left there, with dry cows, as free as the wandering buffalo? Why didn't the rustlers take them along? Even with the brand that could not be altered, those steers and dry cows would make dandy beef.

That question he put to Steve one day. It was not answered—he scarcely expected it would be. But a new look had come into Steve's eyes, Wylie noticed. From deep unmitigated gloom Steve's attention had been caught and held with a new idea, so far as Wylie could guess. It was as though Steve had suddenly stopped worrying and settled down to straight, clear thinking.

It was nothing definite, nothing Wylie could lay his finger upon, but it was there. Steve was no fool. Maybe he would study the thing out and find the right answer. It was high time somebody did, thought Wylie, and rode the south line with his eyes turned expectantly toward the Whoop-up trail where a cloud of dust might herald the coming of Moon and Davis any day, now, and he whistled cheerfully as he rode.

Chapter Twenty-Five: STEVE BROODS

ONE DAY AFTER DINNER, when the cowboys had saddled fresh horses and betaken themselves to the hills, Steve and Wylie stretched themselves out in the shade of the bunkhouse to smoke and rest a while before they too went forth to ride.

Lying on his back with his big hat tilted down over his nose, Wylie's brain once more took up the endless circling around the rustling. From under his lowered lids he watched Steve brooding over his cigarette, staring straight before him with the blank, unseeing gaze of one whose thoughts are focused intently upon something far distant from the scene before his eyes. Steve had one little habit of making a small throat-clearing noise back near his palate when he was close to the answer to some puzzling question, a whispered "ahem" when he was "getting warm." He was making that sound now. When he was sure that he had it, he would turn and give Wylie a sharp, boring glance, and abruptly he would begin talking, making the thing plain as the nose on your face.

A tingle of expectation swept Wylie's nerves. Old Steve was figuring it out, Wylie would have sworn. You couldn't say a word now. You had to let him strictly alone and wait.

Wylie waited. Fell asleep, lying there watching the cold, half-burned cigarette tilted rakishly downward from the corner of Steve's mouth.

A medley of voices woke him. He sat up rubbing his eyes, just in time to see Dave Spellman and the Roman Four horse-wrangler swing down from their horses ten feet away.

"Howdy, people," Dave greeted them jauntily. "How's everything?"

"Oh, just so-so," Wylie answered, yawning as he got up and dusted off his pants. "I reckon you could eat."

"That's what brought me high-tailing into camp," Dave laughed. "Happened to come across the river looking for a little bunch of horses that's been running on the flat opposite Kismet. Pretty dry, and the grass is fed down close, and the horses have moved outa there. I've been hunting 'em over this way—so I just moseyed on over with the full intention of holding up that Mexican and getting a square meal."

The horse-wrangler disappeared into the cabin to tell Juan he had a hungry man to feed, and when he returned he volunteered to take Dave's horse to the stable and feed him.

"I heard you fellows have been riding down river," Dave observed when he had his smoke going. "Get any cattle?"

"Not a hoof," Wylie confessed ruefully. "The boys went down fifty miles or more."

"Thought you wouldn't have much luck. We didn't, I know. Too rough for rustlers, even. We've been doing some tall riding on the north side, ourselves," Dave told them. "We combed every foot of the range over there, and still we're shy a heap of cattle."

"Same here, Dave. Got any theories to pass along?"

Dave shook his head. "The other day I run across Dick in Kismet, full as a lord. Just happened he was in one of his friendly spells when everybody looks like his long-lost brother. I tried my damnedest to pump him." He gave another slow shake of the head. "I'd hate to think he was mixed up in any crooked work, even if he is hand-in-glove with the Lightning. But he's a throwback, in our family. No telling what he might be up to.

"Anyway, I did my darnedest to get around on his sunny side, and by knocking the Roman Four a little I thought maybe he'd loosen up and say something that'd give me a clue. It didn't work, though. Beyond a few hints about what Pike could do to you fellows— and the KM too, for that matter—he never let out a word."

"He was kind enough to inform Steve and me," Wylie said dryly, "that the Lightning would strike us one of these days, and what was left of the Roman Four wouldn't make a grease spot in hell. Or words to that effect. Ain't that right, Steve?"

Steve, sitting on his boot heels with that same blank, speculative stare in his eyes, looked up and nodded grimly. He sighed, hunched himself into a more comfortable position against the bunkhouse wall, and reaching into his coat pocket brought forth an old envelope and began making aimless marks upon it with his tally pencil. Like his whispery throat-clearing, this too was an old trick of Steve's when he wanted to think. Wylie gave him a shrewd, appraising glance, feeling again that secret stirring of hope. Let him alone, and old Steve would find the answer.

"Big Bill Longbow told me you fellows had quite a ruckus with Dick," Dave went on, his eyes idly following the movements of Steve's pencil. "Bill says you come near sending Dick over the high divide. I told yuh Dick was a sure enough trouble-hunter. You want to watch out when you're in Dick's neighborhood, both you boys. Dick's worse than an Injun for holding a grudge. He'd wait ten years, if he had to, for a chance to play even." He pinched out the fire from his cigarette. "It'll pay you and Steve both to have eyes in the back of your heads if you aim to stop on this range."

"We ain't plannin' on pullin' out, for him or no one else," Steve retorted brusquely without looking up.

"Well, I'd sure hope not. That is, if you want to stay. But I'll tell yuh right now that if things go on like they have in the past couple of years, I'll hunt myself another range—if I've got enough cattle left to need one. Any cow outfit can generally manage a plain case of rustling, but this mysterious disappearing of cattle I don't *sabe*. And unless I can get a line that can be followed up, I'm through."

"We hate mysteries, ourselves." Steve raised gloomy eyes to rest briefly upon Dave. "We hate it so damn bad we're going to camp right here till we run this one out into the open and read its brand." He crumpled the envelope into a ball and tossed it from him, getting to his feet as Juan thrust out his head and called musically that dinner was ready for Señor Spellman.

"Well, here's hoping we all don't go broke first, old timer," Dave made sardonic answer, moving toward the cabin. "I sure would be willing to lend a hand at the final ceremonies, if I'm in the country when it happens."

"Chances are you will be," grunted Steve, and followed Wylie to the corral, to saddle their horses and get ready to join the boys.

A whirling dust devil at that moment swept across the yard, caught Dave Spellman's hat, and spun it toward a clump of weeds. Dave went after it with long steps and caught it where it sat brim to the ground. Dusting off his hat with his elbow and slaps against his leg, Dave went in and ate a very good dinner, afterward riding with Steve and Wylie to the lower end of the coulee and there leaving them to make his way home, whistling cheerfully as he rode out of sight.

Chapter Twenty-Six: A FOOL FOR WORRY

KIRK LATIMER WAS GIVING A LAST PULL at his latigo next morning, with a wary eye on his horse, which betrayed a secret urge to set his teeth in his master's left arm, when Steve Tilton came quietly up and stood just behind Kirk's shoulder.

"You needn't mount just yet, Kirk," he said in a low, confidential tone. "Let the boys start off without yuh. You and me will take a ride by ourselves today. Better go have Juan put us up some sandwiches. It's liable to be an all-day trip."

"What's up, Steve?" asked Wylie, who was leading his horse out of the corral and had chanced to overhear that last sentence.

"Oh, nothing much." Steve looked slightly put out. "I've got a notion I've maybe figured out the answer, is all. Me and Kirk'll go on a still hunt of our own, just to see if I'm right. No use gettin' the boys all stirred up till we know for shore." Steve turned away as if the subject were closed.

"Well, hold on a minute! What's the matter with my going along? If you've got something—"

Steve gave him a sour look of dissent. "Trail herd's liable to be here any minute now, almost. It's your place to be on hand so's you can tell 'em what we've been up against. This ain't no war party, Wylie. Me and Kirk is goin' to prowl around a little by ourselves, that's all. Few things I want to check up on."

Wylie followed him. "What is it you've got next to, Steve?" he persisted. "I noticed you were doing some tall old studying, yesterday afternoon. What you got on your mind?"

Steve hesitated, then pulled his eyebrows down in a scowl. "Wait till I come back and I'll tell yuh—mebby. I ain't goin' off half-cocked, this time. We've had too damn much of that all spring." He turned away, picked up his bridle reins, and lifted one foot to the stirrup. "You keep yer shirt on and yer mouth shut. I'll mebby have plenty to say when we git back tonight. And mebby I won't. All depends."

He was in the saddle, reining away from his partner like a stranger. Wylie lifted his shoulders in a shrug of angry acceptance.

"The original clam!" he snorted as he swung limberly into the saddle. But Wylie Brooks was not a sullen young man by nature, and ten steps away he looked back over his shoulder.

"I've got a hunch that trail herd will be kicking dust down over the hill before dark," he called cheerfully. "Me, I'm going to ride south today—pilot 'em in to camp."

Steve retorted, "Well, I've got a hunch of my own. You foller yourn and I'll take mine. Tell them rannies I'll have a job for 'em t'morra."

More than that he would not say, though Wylie held in his horse hoping for a further hint of what Steve had in mind. But the two rode off without a word or a glance in his direction, and he was forced to carry this new mystery with him up over the ridge and out upon the range to the south.

All day he puzzled over it while he rode the high ridges keeping watch for the far-off gray dust clouds that would herald the coming of the herds, and turning back the scattered little groups of IV cattle that showed a disposition to wander away from Cathedral Butte range. So carefully was the Roman Four watching the stock that their line riding was practically day-herding. All day, and sometimes far into the evening, the IV riders might be seen jogging toward some pinnacle where a clear view might be had over miles of country. The thief must be bold indeed and cloaked withal in a mantle of invisibility if he would help himself to IV cattle now.

In the long afterglow which follows sunset in the

northern latitudes Wylie rode into camp, and his eyes went first to the place where Steve always left his saddle. It was not there, nor was Kirk's. As long as there was any hope of seeing trail dust he had lingered on the range, sure that Kirk and Steve would be home ahead of him—or half convincing himself of his certainty that they would be there. And they were not, nor any sign of them.

It didn't mean a thing, he argued mentally. He was late himself. In a country like this, rough and empty and only your own guess to say how many miles you traveled, a man was likely to keep going and never think about having to cover all that territory again, getting home. They'd come, all right. Two wise old birds like them. . . .

Nevertheless he swallowed his warmed-over supper with little relish. The boys who had been line riding east and north hadn't seen a thing of Kirk and Steve, nor had the two who patrolled the range over toward the Lightning. He thought he could detect a certain uneasiness in their voices, but then he told himself that they were merely reflecting his own. He was letting Steve get on his nerves.

Steve was older, wiser in the ways of the range, but that could not justify his sullen way of keeping things to himself. They were full partners; as a matter of fact it was Wylie's money that had started them in the cattle business for themselves—and Wylie was no tenderfoot, either. He had taken his share of the work as it came, held up his end from the very start. It was all right and fine for a man to know how to keep his mouth shut, Wylie grumbled mentally as he smoked his after-supper cigarette outside in the dusk, but when two men were partners there should be no secrets between them, especially in a matter that concerned them equally. Say what you would, Steve Tilton was carrying his reticence too far.

While the nighthawks swooped and called lonesomely in the dusk, Wylie sat out by the cabin door and waited. Once he thought he saw Steve and Kirk riding up along the creek, and started eagerly for the corral to meet them and swear amiably at the two for staying so long. But when he came closer he saw that it was only a couple of loose horses ambling along in the shadows, and with a queer sinking sensation at the pit of his stomach he turned and went back to his post beside the cabin door.

From the bunkhouse came the murmur of voices as the men talked sleepily of the small happenings of the day. They were not worrying about Steve and Kirk, that was certain. Behind him came the rattle of pots and pans, Juan singing a Spanish love song under his breath while he busied himself and kept the coffee hot for his other boss. Cutting across the plaintive melody in the cabin, a coyote off on the hillside set up a querulous yapping, working himself into a clamor worthy a full pack.

Then the moon swept a luminous brush across the eastern skyline, followed its light, and rested its huge yellow rim for a moment upon the hilltop as if it were peering down into the coulee before it started its long leisurely journey across the purple arc of the sky. Good riding for the boys, Wylie thought. They'd keep along in the shadows, seeing without being seen. They might run onto something if they were quiet enough. Maybe that was what kept them so long; maybe Steve had counted on the moon, had cached himself somewhere in the dark to wait and watch some suspected spot.

Heartened by that surmise, Wylie sat watching the pale radiance slide farther and farther down the steep slope of the Butte. As clear as day he saw it, with black patches where boulders lay or rock ledges jutted out. Yes, old Steve was foxy, all right. Picked his cover and would watch all night, probably.

Juan came out of the cabin, his dark face lighted by the moon. "Stove, she's shut up tight, coffee she's keep hot two, t'ree hour. Supper is in oven. Me, I'm sleep now?"

"Sure, Juan. I don't reckon they'll show up till daybreak, now. You go on to bed."

"Buenas noches, señor," Juan grinned, making fun of the little formality which he secretly loved to show even though he would be laughed at for his pains.

"Good night, Juan. I'll take a look at the fire before I turn in."

Long black shadow sliding before him, Juan walked to the bunkhouse, stood for a minute to take in the serene beauty of the night, suddenly disappeared within. Wylie finished the cigarette he was smoking, ground out the fire from the stub under his heel, spat on it for good measure, and stood up stretching and yawning as tense nerves relaxed. Steve and Kirk were all right—trust old Steve to look out for his own hide!

He went in and pushed another stick of sagebrush into the stove, then went to bed. The days were long, and this one had been stretched far beyond its normal limit. The rest of the outfit had been asleep for two hours or more. He would have been, if he weren't such a fool for worrying.

Five minutes after his head struck the pillow, Wylie Brooks was down on the Brazos with a girl in his arms who promised again that she would wait until he had a nice home ready for her up north.

Chapter Twenty-Seven: NIGHT PROWLER

SOMETIME IN THE NIGHT Wylie sat up in his bed and listened. Save for a gentle snore in the near-by bunkhouse, the sound rumbling in through the open window beside his bed, the camp was still. By the feeling of emptiness in the cabin he was certain Steve had not come back. Something had wakened him, however. Worried though he might be, his nerves were too healthy to play tricks on him like this, snatching him out of a sound sleep to sit up and listen.

Ears strained for some sound to come again, he waited. Nothing seemed to be moving outside, and not even a mosquito hummed in the cabin. But to make sure he got up and struck a match, held it aloft and looked around.

Steve's bunk was empty, just as he knew it would be. Through the open door that led into the next room he could see the long kitchen table set with places for two, a cheerless foreboding scene in that flickering light. The match went out. Wylie held the charred end in his fingers while he listened again.

There was no sound. Vaguely uneasy, he sat down on his bunk and fumbled on the box beside him for smoking-materials with the cigarette he had rolled and laid handy in case he woke and wanted a smoke. He had it well going, felt the soothing effect of it easing his tension, was calling himself an old granny, when through the open window there came to his ears, faint but unmistakable, the creak of saddle leather, the muffled hoofbeats of a horse moving off at a walk.

That puzzled him. Steve and Kirk would not be likely to ride past the cabins on their way to the corral —they would come up the coulee instead of down. He got up and thrust his head out through the window. The moon, having passed the cloud that hid it for a while, now shone brightly, high overhead, shrinking all shadows to narrow black margins. Yet he could see nothing move, and though he listened long he heard no further sound.

He had finished his smoke and was about to turn in again, when halfway up the lower slope of Cathedral Butte he saw something moving out from the narrow strip of black shade that fringed a row of quaking aspens. It emerged into white moonlight, then disappeared behind a huge square boulder, climbing the deep-worn buffalo trail which went round the Butte to a ridge that led off to the north, the trail Pike Stoddard had taken that first Sunday when Wylie had met him as he came down off the Butte.

Eyebrows drawn close together, he stared intently, waiting for another clear view. It was a man on horseback—he would have sworn to that. What he was a little slower to realize was that he knew the horse, and that the humped figure in the saddle was also familiar. In a moment the rider showed again on an open stretch of the moonlit trail, and Wylie's last doubt fled. The horse was the white pacer which Pike Stoddard rode, and Pike was on him, riding away from the Roman Four.

"Playing lookout, hunh?" Wylie snorted. "Well, I'll just drop you a gentle hint that night prowlers get what they have coming to 'em, around here!"

On two pegs driven into the wall above Wylie's bed rested a Sharps rifle. It was heavy, with a long, old-fashioned barrel, and it looked as if it had long seen its best days, but it could drive a bullet through a buffalo at half a mile. He took it down, slipped a cartridge into the chamber, and laid the barrel across the window sill.

The white horse had passed behind a huddle of piled boulders, but unless it stopped and stood there it must show again in the open space beyond. Wylie held a little high, just over the trail where it showed above the rocks. His finger tightened on the trigger. He wanted old Pike to hear that big slug sing its song in passing.

With the heavy vicious roar of a stick of dynamite the old gun bellowed into the night. Echoes awoke and flung the sound far up and down the creek bottom. Before these died in murmurings the bunkhouse spewed forth armed men clad only in their underwear but with gun barrels gleaming blue and silver in the moonlight.

"What's the matter?" Rock Sellers's voice cried sharply. "Who was that shootin'?"

"That was me, Rock," Wylie called ungrammatically, already half ashamed of the excitement he had

caused. "I was just saying howdy to the big chief of
the Lightning. He—"

"Did yuh git 'em?" Sorry cried eagerly.

"I hope not. All I wanted was to dust his heels and
let him know we sleep with one eye open down here.
Saw him on the trail, riding away from here, and from
the way he jumped his horse down into the shade I
reckon he got my message, all right."

"You'd orta killed the old buzzard!" Sorry grumbled.
"What business has he got over here in the middle o'
the night?"

"No business. He *sabes* that now." Wylie laughed
shortly. "Get back to bed, boys. I reckon that's all for
tonight."

"Why don't we take in after 'im and call fer a showdown, and have it over with?" Rock lingered to urge.
"Him comin' over here in the middle of the night ain't
for no good, and you can gamble on that."

"Maybe not, but he was alone and he didn't do a
thing but prowl. We'll wait till Steve gets back, and
see what he says. Go on, Rock. Get you some sleep."

For a long while after Rock left him, Wylie sat with
his arms folded on the window sill, watching the trail
and listening for hoofbeats. Then he yawned, shivered
in the chill that comes before dawn, and crawled into
his blankets. He slept too soundly for dreams, though
just as he was drifting off into unconsciousness he
found himself picturing exactly how old Pike Stoddard
would look swinging by the neck from a big cottonwood limb. He had a startlingly clear vision of the
white horse dropping its rump under the stroke of a
quirt in Steve's hand, and galloping off a few rods only

to stop and turn to stare back in bewilderment at his master left dangling.

"One rustler less," he thought Steve exclaimed in his surliest tone. And that was all he remembered.

Chapter Twenty-Eight: "THE LIGHTNING HAS STRUCK."

A SHRILL YELL charged with a nameless horror brought Wylie out of bed in one leap which left him standing half awake in the middle of the room. Somehow the old Sharps rifle was in his hands, half-aimed through the window. Then he snapped into full consciousness, saw that gray dawn had come, the sky showing faint streaks of color from the sunrise just beginning to approach. Steve had not come. At least his bed was as he had spread the blankets smooth yesterday morning. From the bunkhouse voices clamored inquiry and answers that told nothing. Booted feet were running.

Something more than the dawn chill set Wylie shaking. Frantically pulling on pants and boots, he snatched up his six-shooter and belt, buckling it as he ran. He must have overslept, he thought, as one does think of trivial things in the midst of a great catastrophe—and this, he knew, was something tragic. The men of the Roman Four did not stampede over small alarms.

Past the corner of the stable, out of sight from the cabins, a little knot was forming, curiously still now that the first alarm had been raised. Behind him feet pounded on the trail as men wakened from sleep in the bunkhouse raced to the scene; Juan ran panting from the kitchen, his floursack apron whipping in the breeze he created.

As he came up to them the stunned half circle of men glanced his way, stepped aside to leave him a clear path. The night-herder, standing in his stirrups and speaking rapidly in a horrified half whisper, settled back in his saddle and was silent, his round eyes wide, staring at Wylie.

Wylie knew all this, sensed the wordless horror of the cowboys, fought it back with his own terrible incredulity as he faced the unthinkable thing before him. For there, suspended from the low ridgepole that jutted out from the gabled end of the log building, his booted, spurred feet no more than a few inches from the ground, dangled Steve Tilton. His face was waxy— not like a hanged man—and in his wide-open eyes, staring straight into Wylie's, was a look of astonished resentment.

"Good God, Steve, who—?" Wylie stopped, aware that he was about to ask a useless question of a dead man. He staggered, suddenly dizzy, his brain whirling inside his skull. Or so he thought at the moment. Then he was sitting down on the tongue of the mess-wagon, and Rock Sellers was holding him by the shoulders. Juan was there, wiping off the neck of a bottle with a corner of his apron. He held it to Wylie's mouth, the glass clicking against his teeth.

"I keep for somet'ing happen," Juan said shakily. "You take big wan. . . . More. . . . One more for sure."

Wylie's lifted wrist struck away the flask. The liquor tasted flat as cold tea, but his spinning brain slowed, steadied, and cleared. Unobtrusively Rock moved to block the view from Wylie's sight.

"Better come on back to the cabin, hadn't yuh?"

Rock said gently. "The boys'll—look after things. Nothin' you kin do, down here."

"The hell I can't!" Against the pressure of Rock's hands Wylie stood up, gave his hat a yank forward. "Take him—lay him on his bed where he belongs." But he kept his face turned from the gruesome figure at the stable end, and he kept his thoughts turned away from his personal loss, from the years when Steve had been to him like an older brother, gruff and contentious at times perhaps, but loyal to the last drop of his blood. He would not think of that. He could not.

"Well, the Lightning has struck, all right," he said, so calmly that Rock gave him a quick look. "Now the Roman Four will see what it can do about building a cyclone of its own."

While the men carefully bore the stiffened body away to the cabin, Wylie forced himself to question the nighthawk who had screeched the alarm. But the shaken herder had little to tell him.

He had brought in the saddle bunch at daybreak, as was his custom, and corralled them without noticing anything wrong. He remembered now that the horses had seemed a little more skittish and snorty than usual, but the air was crimpy and he laid it to their being cold. It was only when he rode past the end of the stable that his horse shied and he discovered the body. Then he yelled.

No, he hadn't heard or seen a thing out of the way, all night, he said, in answer to a final question. Wylie nodded. The saddle horses had been grazing in an arm of the coulee, across the creek and back toward the hills. It would have been impossible for the herder to see or hear anything that went on at the ranch buildings. He would not even be able to see the trail up around Cathedral Butte.

Wylie left him and walked slowly up to the bunkhouse where the men had gathered in a group ominously quiet, talking in low tones that grated with the killing rage held in leash. Kirk's name was spoken as he came near, then they looked at him and fell silent.

"The Lightning has struck," he repeated calmly. "Just as Dick Spellman threatened it would. This thing was done to stampede us—drive us outa the country. They scared those nesters, a few years back, and they think they can scare us. And that's where they're fooled.

"This thing has come to a showdown. It's gone past cattle stealing, boys. From now on it's a case of kill or die. And for my part I'd rather go out like a white man, with my boots on and a hot gun in my hand, than wait and be shot down from behind by a sneaking cow thief."

"You're damn' tootin'!"

"The law gives every man a right to defend himself and his property. We can't play a waiting game any longer, boys—we've got to go in and clean up the bunch that did this to us. There's Kirk—they got him, too, I reckon. But I'm going to leave it up to you fellows. Shall we wait for those trail herds, Davis and Len Moon and the boys?"

"Not a damn' minute! They'd orter been here by now. We'll kill our own snakes, Wylie."

"You lead the way and we'll foller you to hell."

"They got ridgepoles at the Lightnin', I reckon.

Time the Roman Four done a little decoratin' too."

Rock Sellers said bitterly, "Steve Tilton was as good a man as ever stood in a stirrup. And me and Kirk growed up together. The quicker we start, the better it'll suit me."

"All right, boys, slap your saddles on your top horses and we'll go, quick as we eat. We've got to keep our heads—and this is liable to be a long, hard day. I wish we knew what's become of Kirk; while he lived and could pull a trigger he never would have let them—do that to Steve." In spite of himself his voice broke at the mention of his partner's name.

The young man named Bill swallowed twice, fumbled his hat, and somehow found the courage to speak what was in his mind:

"One thing, Wylie—I dunno as it helps much—but Steve wasn't—Steve passed out with a bullet in his heart. He wasn't hung. Not till afterward, anyway. I helped pack 'im inside and I took p'ticular notice.

"Steve was shot from behind and the bullet come out over his heart. The hangin' was jest a scary play they made at us, Wylie. He was dead long before that rope went round his neck. I know fer shore."

"Thanks, Bill." Wylie's teeth clamped hard together. "That—helps."

It did, immeasurably. As the men went off to saddle their horses they talked with less restraint, as if Bill's statement had relieved a tension among them. Shooting was bad enough, but it was the way many a good man went out in those grim days. They could accept that as the misfortune of range war. They would miss old Steve, they would avenge him, no mistake about that.

But it was a great relief to know he did not die in the horrible fashion they had thought—that he had not died hanging from the ridgepole of his own stable.

But there was Kirk unaccounted for. Maybe the Lightning had him, was holding him alive for some reason. They would have thought it a bigger joke to hang the two together, though, throw a bigger scare into the Roman Four. Maybe Kirk got away—and yet they knew better than to think he would ever quit a friend. He had shown his mettle too often. And he was fond of Steve.

They were still discussing Kirk's absence when Juan's drumming on a tin pan called them all to breakfast.

Chapter Twenty-Nine: HELL-BENT FOR HANGING

SUCH WAS THEIR HASTE and so perfunctory their attempt at eating breakfast, the sun was no more than half an hour above the skyline when ten somber-faced riders turned their backs upon the Roman Four and headed their horses toward the Lightning ranch. From the cabin doorway Juan, left alone to guard their dead, stared longingly up the coulee for some minutes after the last horseman had disappeared on the trail where Pike Stoddard had dodged a bullet not many hours before.

Juan would have given a year's wages, and that eagerly, for the privilege of buckling on his gun and following the cowboys on that early-morning ride. But Steve, lying so quietly on his bunk with his blanket pulled over his head, must not be left alone. Juan sighed heavily and turned back to his dishwashing, stepping softly as if he feared waking his boss lying in the next room.

Spurs jingling faintly, saddles creaking with the whispery sound all riders know well and secretly love to hear, the Roman Four men rode without much speech. Once Rock Sellers turned himself in the saddle and gazed back at the flaming new-risen sun as if he wondered how many of them—including himself first of all—would see that sun dip down over the mountains that evening.

Once Wylie pulled in his horse on a high point in the trail and looked back through a gap in the hills, to the level range to the south, and seeing that, others halted to look speculatively toward the south. There was no need to say why. Every man knew.

But there was no gray cloud hanging low on the skyline—no sign yet of the trail herds. And then the wild broken hills swallowed them and shut off the last glimpse of open range behind. They rode forward eagerly, spurring their horses up the slopes, anxious for the fight to come.

Five miles or so from the southernmost line of Lightning pasture fence a little skit of dust flung up out of a hollow caught their wary glance. As one man the Roman Four riders straightened in their saddles, hitching gun-belts into place while their eyes fixed with squinting intent gaze upon that telltale, speeding gray banner of dust.

"Might be Kirk comin' home," Rock hazarded without much hope in his voice, and was the first to jump his horse forward in a gallop. Wylie beside him kept pace, the rest thundering after.

On the first rise Wylie threw up his hand to stay his riders, and pulled his own horse to a stand. From the gray cloud boiling across the flat below them a horseman emerged as the breeze shifted, blowing the dust behind him. A brown horse, strange to them all, loped steadily toward the group—and the wiry figure humped forward in the saddle was old Pike Stoddard himself.

The boys of the Roman Four loosened the guns in their holsters and rode forward in a thin skirmish line, eyes searching this way and that, suspicious of treachery, ambush, whatever Indian trick old Pike might devise. Not even Wylie spoke a word of warning nor gave an order. These were seasoned men—they knew what chance they took, knew exactly what was to be done. And without any deliberate thought upon the subject they nevertheless managed to look as deadly as a painted war party descending upon a lone white man in the wilderness.

Still Pike Stoddard rode indomitably forward as if bent on suicide. They did not charge down upon him in a whirlwind rush. They hurried less than he, yet their very deliberation had an implacable quality that must have chilled the blood of the old man, tough as he was.

Ten rods lay between them—five—two. Then Wylie kicked his horse ahead, coolly ranged alongside the Lightning boss and leaning sidewise plucked the six-shooter from its holster on Pike's hip. Stoddard's keen gray eyes, the color of lead and hard as bullets, watched the group unblinkingly from under his shaggy, sand-colored brows. If he felt any uneasiness over the situation in which he found himself he did not show it by so much as the flicker of an eyelash. From his manner this was the accepted form of greeting, a ceremony commonly observed when neighboring cowmen met on the range.

Wylie Brooks ended the silence, a nervous impatience betrayed in his voice, though his face was calm enough.

"We were headed for your place, Stoddard. We want to show you something. It won't be news to you, and the chances are you left it yourself last night. Just the same, you're going back with us and take a look."

Pike Stoddard folded his hands on the saddle horn and spat tobacco juice off to one side away from the slow breeze.

"Just as yuh say, Brooks. I was on my way over to have a talk with yuh, anyway. We could do it here an' save time, but if you'd ruther go on back an' have it there, it's all the same to me."

Wylie's face flushed a little, then settled to its hard mask again. "Aren't you breaking the rule you Lightning killers seem to have made? This daylight riding of yours I'm afraid I don't quite *sabe*. What's the idea?"

"Ain't got time to chaw the rag over what time of day or night I ride. I got just one rule, Brooks, and that's to ride when an' where I damn please an' my business calls me. Right now I've got some business with the Roman Four."

"You're damn right you have! We aimed to transact it over at the Lightning, where I hear there's ridgepoles that need decorating bad. But first I want you at the Roman Four."

"Hmph." Pike Stoddard's hard eyes moved in a sweeping glance around the group. "Mebby you know what you're drivin' at, but I doubt it. Loony talk as I ever heard. What's all this tommyrot about Lightnin' ridgepoles? Hey?" He gave Wylie a hard appraising stare. "What's all this you been hearin' about my ridgepoles?"

"Nothing much. Only it seems there's a new fashion come into the country. The thing is to go decorate your neighbor's ridgepole in the night when everybody's asleep. Idea is to surprise 'em next morning when they get up. The Roman Four aims to keep up with the times, that's all."

"If that's the case, what yuh doin' over here after sun-up?" Old Pike's jaws worked fast, and he spat again.

"Giving you fair warning, which is more'n you gave the Roman Four," Wylie flashed back at him.

Pike turned his quid of tobacco to the other cheek, shaking his head slowly from left to right. He scanned again the hostile faces of the Roman Four men, brought his gaze back to Wylie.

"I'd like to know what you think you're talkin' about, Brooks," he said finally. "All this hintin' around about decoratin' ridgepoles in the night an' so-on, I don't know a thing about. Plumb mystery to me."

Wylie flushed again and he edged his horse nearer as if he meant to strike the old man from the saddle. "I suppose you don't know a thing about sneakin' over to our place last night, either! I don't suppose you remember a thing about duckin' lead up on the Butte trail! That's all a mystery too, I reckon!"

Pike looked at him, and for the first time a shade of emotion crept into his face. "Yeah, I rode over there last night," he said calmly enough. "No law ag'in that, and I don't make no bones about it. Somebody fired a shot at me as I was leavin'. Damn pore shot, he was."

"I'd have been better if I'd known then what your errand was," gritted Wylie. "So you do know what I'm talkin' about! You know why we aim to hang you and all your damned thieving cutthroats to your own ridgepoles as fast as we can string you up! You started the fashion, by God, and we'll follow it till we run out of rope!"

A strange look came into Pike's eyes as he listened. "Now, now, look here," he expostulated in an amazingly conciliatory tone. "I ain't goin' to argue about all you folks aim to do. You're two-to-one and you'd git away with it easy enough, fur as that goes. Go ahead an' clean up the Lightnin' if you're bound to; there's only five men back there now, countin' the cook. But that feller you sent over to rep with us las' spring, he's down at the ranch and he wants t' have a talk with you boys. That's what—"

"Kirk Latimer? You mean to tell me you've got him?"

Old Pike nodded. "That there's what I was comin' over to tell yuh. He's—"

Rock Sellers spurred forward, shouldering Pike's horse toward Wylie. "What's that you say? You got Kirk Latimer?" He pulled himself together, forced a grin that contorted his face to a murderous mask. "Lemme tell you this, old man. If you've harmed or hurt Kirk Latimer by so much as a scratch, you'll hang by your heels instead of your damn dirty neck!"

"You keep yore shirt on, young feller," Pike calmly advised him. He took out a plug of tobacco, looked it over, cleared his mouth of the discarded quid and prepared to pry off a new one, pausing in the operation to glance from Rock to Wylie. "You don't need to worry none about Kirk Latimer. He's shot up consid'able, but he's tough and liable to pull through all right."

He took his bite of tobacco, looked at Wylie again. "Quick as he come to his senses he commenced pesterin' me to send fer you. Got quite consid'able on his mind he wants t' tell yuh. He was in such a dang hurry, wouldn't hardly leave me time to swaller my breakfast after I told him I'd ride over m'self and have a talk with yuh.

"Course, you kin suit yerselves, but if you take my advice you'll come on back with me and have a talk with Kirk. Pay yuh, in the long run. Time enough to start in afterward and do all that hangin' you was makin' your brags about."

Wrinkles showed around his eyes, new ones appearing among the old. He was squinting into the sun, watching the Roman Four riders exchange glances of mute inquiry. When he looked away his hard old mouth was puckered as if he wanted to smile.

Chapter Thirty: EASY PICKINGS

WYLIE BROOKS WAS THE FIRST TO SPEAK, and his voice betrayed the strain of mixed emotions:

"Look here, Stoddard, if you're saying this to get us over to your place, thinking you'll double-cross us, you'll be the sorriest old man in the country. If it's straight goods, the best thing you can do is go on and tell us the rest, and cut all this hinting and mystery. We've stood about all we're going to, from the Lightning or any other outfit." He drew a sharp breath, getting himself in hand again. But his eyes never left old Pike Stoddard's face.

"You know what happened. The whitest man that ever threw a leg over a saddle was shot down like a beef critter last night, and then brought home and strung up like a horse thief on the ridgepole of his own stable. With him laid out waiting to be buried, we ain't in the mood for any argument or any beating around the bush with the Lightning. The men that did that to Steve Tilton are going to get the same medicine they gave him. I'm telling you that straight to your face, Pike. I saw you riding away from the ranch last night. And if I'd known then what brought you over, I'd have pulled down closer with that old Sharps. I can tell you that."

Pike Stoddard freed his mouth of tobacco juice. "Well, I still say yuh better wait an' see that man of yourn that's down to my place. You boys have a talk with him, and then you go ahead accordin' to your own judgment. If hangin' me is all that's goin' to satisfy yuh, go right ahead an' string me up. You're ten to our five. I ain't countin' m'self, seein' you aim to make me the hangee, and you got my gun so I couldn't do nothin' if I wanted to."

To the questions flung at him by Wylie and Rock, the old man merely shook his head.

"You shore are the time-wastin'est outfit I ever seen

in m'life," he complained. "Settin' here gabbin' on a
pinnacle when you oughta be foggin' down there to
see your man. Go talk to Kirk Latimer. You wouldn't
b'lieve nothin' I said if I was to set here an' talk all
day."

"You're damn right we wouldn't!" snapped Wylie.
"Ride on back, then. And don't make any false motions, or we'll snake you in to the Lightning corral at
the end of a rope."

At the Lightning, they swept into the ranch yard
at a gallop, old Pike Stoddard in their midst with his
hands tied to the saddle horn, his jaws moving with a
leisurely rhythm over a stale quid of tobacco. Guns in
hand, they shouted for all and sundry to come out into
the open, and for a minute or two not a man showed
himself.

"Might as well humor 'em, boys," old Pike called in
his hard tone, which though quiet would carry far.
"Come on out here, all of yuh. The Roman Four is on
the warpath this morning."

Wylie gave him a sidelong, suspicious glance, but
Pike Stoddard was calmly watching his men walk out
into the sunlit yard and stand impassively while certain of the Roman Four men dismounted and searched
them for weapons—and found none.

"That ain't all," Pike dryly informed them. "You
ain't rounded up the cook, yet."

So the cook was brought from the kitchen to stand
with the rest while soft bread dough dried on his hairy
arms.

"Your man is layin' in there in the bunkhouse."
Pike nodded toward the low building that had pro-

duced three of the four Lightning cowboys.

Without a word Wylie and Rock swung off their horses and started for the cabin, four others at their heels walking warily, guns ready, looking for treachery. Wylie glanced back, remembering something.

"Untie Stoddard and let him come along," he said, and waited until Pike joined the group and took the lead. They followed him into a large room where Kirk Latimer's voice greeted them with evident relief at their arrival.

"Hello, cowboys! Shore am glad you showed up so quick. Pike must of hit the high places, gittin' to the Roman Four. Now, maybe you'll be able to do some business. Steve—"

"We know about that," Wylie cut him short.

"Yuh *know?*" Kirk's feverish glance swung toward old Pike. "Oh, I reckon yuh do, at that."

"Not from him. They brought Steve home and hung him to our stable last night. He was found this morning. What we want to know is how it happened. And how bad are yuh hurt, Kirk? How does it come you're lying here at the Lightning?" Wylie hooked a bench forward and sat down beside the bunk. "Nothing seems to tie in with anything else. What's the meaning, Kirk?"

Kirk was scowling over some thought of his own. "The gall of them killers—bringin' Steve right to the ranch!" he muttered. Then he looked up at his boss. "Didn't Pike tell yuh?"

"Only that you was here and wanted to have a talk with us. We thought it was a frame-up. Nobody was in the humor to listen to any of Pike's explanations."

Wylie sent an oblique glance up at the old man.

"I wasn't explainin' to these catamounts." Pike grinned sourly. "Not whilst they was so hell-bent fer hangin' on sight. Only thing stopped 'em from hangin' me right then and there, I reckon, was the lack of limbs."

"Yes, and we've still got a strong leaning that way," Wylie retorted. "Damn it, the Roman Four can't stand chewing the rag, with Steve—"

"Well, put another piller in under my head, and I'll tell all I know about it," Kirk said. "I'm weak as a newborn calf. There's a hole in my side you could poke yer thumb into, Wylie." He shot a side glance at Stoddard. "Wasn't struck by Lightnin' that time, either," he drawled.

"Who was it, Kirk?" Wylie stooped to lift the man up.

"Wait till I tell yuh," groaned Kirk, his dark head drooping against Wylie's arm as Rock thrust in place the dingy pillow borrowed from a near-by bunk, where the four other boys were sitting in a solemn-faced row, passing smoking-material down the line as they watched old Pike and listened carefully to every word spoken.

Settled as comfortably as possible, Kirk began again. "Me an' Steve started out on a trail Steve had figured out—and she was a dandy, once yuh knowed. Plain as the nose on yer face, Wylie. Bunch of old cowmen like us, they shore fooled us plenty!

"Anyway, we crossed the river at a place down below the ford. The KM uses it when the water ain't too high. And we prowled around on the north side—"

Wylie started perceptibly. "The north side, eh? How did Steve find out about that other crossing?"

"Jest figured it out, I reckon. He didn't say. He's had a hunch for some time back, but he wouldn't say nothin' till he was shore. You know old Steve. Oh, we was easy game, all right! Picked us like an old woman picks her geese in moltin' time. Got us right down to wing an' tail feathers 'fore we let out the first squawk. Old Steve, he figured it out—but he wanted to make dead shore—and minute he *was* shore, they got 'im!" Kirk's eyes were too bright. He was rambling when he should have been brief and direct.

"I don't quite get yuh, old timer," Wylie leaned closer to say. "You don't—do you mean—"

"I'll show you fellers what he means," old Pike said abruptly. He took a stubby pencil from his pocket and drew a series of short lines on the white canvas tarp that covered the bed. The four on the other bunk got up and came to look over the bowed shoulders of Rock and Wylie. When old Pike's pencil was lifted from the tarp they swore softly.

The wounded man craned his neck down and sidewise to see. "That's it!" He made uncertain, stabbing motions with a nicotined forefinger. "That's what I been tellin' yuh. Steve, he figured it out, but he wouldn't say nothin' till he was shore. An' when he was shore they killed 'im. Come damn near killin' me, too. I'm tougher 'n Steve, I reckon. Easy pickin's—"

Pike Stoddard got up, let his bleak, lead-colored eyes move from man to man.

"I want you should hear your own man tell it," he said grimly. "Gittin' a mite flighty, right now. I'll go git 'im somethin' to take that fever down a notch b'fore he tries to go on talkin'. Keep 'im still, now. I'll be right back."

He turned and walked out, leaving the Roman Four men staring at one another.

Chapter Thirty-One: SHOT IN THE BACK

"ROCK, YOU MAY AS WELL CALL IN the rest of the boys," Wylie muttered without turning his eyes away from Kirk's hot, anxious face. "This is going to be worse than I thought it was. I reckon the Lightning ain't in on the deal, after all. Our mistake. You tell the boys all we know so far, and when Kirk's feeling a little better we'll get the rest of the story."

"It'll be a jim-dandy," Rock predicted as he turned to go. " 'Pears to me we're liable to have our work cut out for us, boss."

"An' that's no dream," Kirk roused himself to declare.

He would have said more had old Pike not come in just then with a hot and bitter brew which he forced Kirk to swallow.

"Wownds ain't serious, either one of 'em," Pike assured the Roman Four men. "Don't b'lieve the bullet that went through his side touched his innards, unless maybe his liver got a nick in it. If he'd of got tended to right when it happened it wouldn't amounted to much."

"That's what I'm in a hurry to hear: how it happened. Soon as he feels able—"

"I'm able as hell," Kirk pettishly declared, still

grimacing over the bitterness of the drink. "Git my mind off that gall tea. Where'd I leave off, Wylie?"

"Where Pike showed us how the brands were worked. How'd you find out?"

"Well, we was over acrost the river, ridin' along the bottom of a brushy canyon right where three forks headed in together. We was workin' back toward the river when they opened up on us from behind a big boulder right up on the aidge of the bank."

"Who? Did you get sight of 'em?"

"Not right then, I didn't. No time to look. A bullet zipped through my shirt sleeve and hit Steve. We was ridin' close together with him just about half a length in the lead, and I seen him fall over on his horse's withers. It jumped and Steve slid off like a bag of barley. I knowed he was dead when he hit the ground, Wylie."

"Through the heart, one of the boys told me."

"Hnh?" Kirk gave a surprised grunt and was about to follow that with a question. Then he remembered and nodded.

"Well, all that happened a damn sight quicker than I kin tell about it. My horse give a big jump when Steve's did, and bolted into the brush 'fore I could pull 'im up. I was goin' back after Steve—don't never think I'd ride off thataway if there was a spark uh life in 'im, Wylie.

"But them bushwhackers was shootin' twigs off'n the bushes all around me. I got down an' snuck up close as I could git to Steve, meanin' to run out an' git 'im back under cover. But it was no use, Wylie. I seen where he was hit, and I knowed the thing to do was git home an' tell you all what the game was."

Wylie answered his anxious stare. "Best thing you ever did in your life, Kirk. You couldn't help Steve any by getting killed yourself."

"Yeah, that's what I figured. He was gone. And you all wouldn't *sabe* how it happened if I didn't hit outa there an' bring word. They kep' down outa sight an' kep' a shootin' into the brush, so I led m' horse along in the thinnest spots where we wouldn't be wigglin' branches an' give ourselves away. If I'd a had m' rifle— but Steve, he never tol' me I was to ride with him till I was saddlin' up, an' I never thought—"

"Take it easy, old timer. You couldn't have saved him."

"I'd a stayed and smoked 'em up some, if I'd had my Winchester. But hell, a six-gun ain't no use in a long-range fight. They kep' their distance, and I could tell they was workin' to git around me and close in." He wagged his hand toward a fruit can of spring water.

Rock it was who held the cold water to Kirk's lips. The wounded man drank thirstily, leaned back with a careful sigh of refreshment. Wylie offered him a fresh-lighted cigarette, but Kirk shook his head.

"Too damn sick to smoke. Where was I? . . . Oh, in the brush dodgin' lead hornets. Well, I piled on my horse and made a dash across an open space into another thicket. I was workin' down the canyon, see; back the way we had come in. They shore smoked me good an' plenty. But I made it and come to a big washout that led into a draw runnin' out from the main canyon. I sneaked up that afoot, leadin' m' horse, an' we made the top without 'em seein' me."

"You always did have any Injun beat for keeping out of sight," Wylie patiently encouraged him. Kirk was indulging a sick man's passion for detail, but he was holding his audience and Wylie would not hurry him. A complete picture of yesterday's tragedy might be useful later on.

"What happened then?"

"Hnh? Oh, yeah. By that time they was shootin' wild and by the sound they was scurrupin' around like dogs huntin' a rabbit. I crawled into a nest uh rocks and got a good look at some of 'em. They thought I was down below in the canyon. They never thought about keepin' their damn backs down outa sight.

"There was one Block Diamond man I've saw in Kismet, an' another feller I didn't know. And two KM punchers—I got a good look at Dave an' Dick Spellman, the dirty—"

Old Pike leaned and spat into a box of ashes. "Dick," his rasping voice interrupted, "drawed some money about a week ago an' pulled out fer Fort Benton. Claimed his back was hurtin' too bad t' do much ridin' an' he was goin' to a doctor. I s'posed that's where he was, the lyin' hound."

Kirk gave a harsh, mirthless laugh that hurt him so much he swore in a whisper until the pain eased.

"He shore as hell didn't ride like his back hurt 'im yestiddy," he commented grimly. "I got 'em about all located as I thought, and clumb on an' hit a long lope toward home. But somebuddy seen me an' raised a whoop an' they all come a-foggin' after me in a bunch."

"Was that when you got hit?"

"No, they never got within gun range. That there

blue roan had a good quarter mile start an' he kep' it. What they done was keep me on the dodge all afternoon, an' I had some close calls. But they never plugged me—not then.

"Well, I didn't think they'd dast foller me plumb into Kismet, so about sundown I cut in toward the river. I was still holdin' m' lead—made damn shore I had 'em all behind me. 'Minded me of that time I got down into 'Pache country—that was 'fore your time, Wylie. I was—"

Without a word Wylie interrupted the impending digression, offering another drink of water. So Kirk came back to the report of yesterday's events.

"Me an' m' horse was both purty well tuckered out an' I was so dry m' tongue was beginnin' to feel like a rolled bacon rind in m'mouth. But I pulled into Kismet all in one piece. Wasn't a soul in sight but ole Bill Longbow. He was settin' out in front smokin' an' takin' life easy.

"So I slides off an' wabbles over to 'im and says I'm about choked. Bill wants to know what's happened, an' if you boys is in trouble or anything. And he gives me a big schooner of beer, best damn beer I ever drunk in m' life. I was kinda oneasy about stoppin' long, but I wanted to let m' horse cool off some 'fore I hit the ford. I was a long ways f'm home, boss, an' I was figurin' on gittin' here with the news—" His febrile gaze clung anxiously to Wylie's face.

"You used your head, Kirk. You always do. I'd have waited a while at Big Bill's, myself. What did they do —go after you right under Longbow's nose?"

"Wait. Lemme tell it as it happened, and I'll git it

straight. You got to know the hull story, er you fellers might mebby git what I got."

"That's what. You go right ahead, Kirk. Tell it your way."

"Well, I had a big schooner of beer, an' Big Bill kep' askin' where I'd been, and was anything wrong at the Roman Four. And I thought mebby they'd be layin' in wait at the ford, and me on a tired horse—anyway, I told Longbow what was up. Told him Dave Spellman was king bee of the rustlers, looked like, and him an' his gang had killed Steve Tilton and was doin' their damnedest to git me. . . . Mebby I was a gabby ole fool, boss, but—"

"I'd have told him, myself. What'd he say?"

"Well, he acted s'prised as hell, Wylie. He couldn't hardly b'lieve Dave was crooked. But he said fer me to hit out fer home, an' if I didn't git word to yuh, he would. He said 'course, I could see the position he's in. He couldn't take sides—him bein' squatted there between fires, yuh might say, an' him with Dolly to pertect till her an' Dick got spliced.

"I told him Dick was in on the killin' and workin' with Dave, an' he jes' shook his head an' tol' me I must be mistaken about that. I didn't have time to argue the point." Kirk grinned wryly. "I looked out and seen their dust. So I tol' Bill to git word to you fellers if I don't make it or he don't hear nothin' from the Roman Four for a day or so, an' he said he'd do that.

"So I got on the roan an' started. Big Bill come an' stood in the doorway, lookin' at the dust about a quarter mile off, an' lookin' at me. An' the last he said to me, boss, was: 'I'm a peaceful man an' all I want is to make me an honest livin', but it looks like all hell is due to pop loose right in front of my door!'"

Chapter Thirty-Two: ROBBERS' ROOST

WYLIE'S HAND SHOOK PERCEPTIBLY as he pinched the fire from his cigarette and tossed the stub out through the open window. He looked at Pike Stoddard, surprising a peculiarly sardonic grin on the old man's face. For a moment his glance remained there, then swung back to Kirk, who was watching him.

"So they followed you this side the river," he summed up Kirk's story. "They sure was bound you wouldn't carry the news into camp. How'd yuh get away, Kirk?"

"Well, I was goin' to tell yuh 'bout that. Want yuh t' git the hull frame-up. Then you c'n lay yer plans. The Lightnin'll throw in with yuh—Pike said so."

"Not till they git the hull story from you," Pike amended. "You'll be outa your head an' talkin' wild if you string it out much longer. You're takin' up time."

"Well, damn it, a sick man's s'posed t' be humored some," Kirk complained. "I might die. I want the boys t' git the hull story complete while I'm at it."

"You go ahead. I *sabe* Big Bill's predicament. He hates to lose customers, that's all. All right, you started for the ford. We've got it that far. Then what?"

"Then I splashes into the ford, spurrin' the roan an' not lettin' him drink till we hit the other side. I didn't want that bunch ridin' up an' start pot-shottin' me whilst I was in the water. Once acrost, I could lay behind a hummock an' stand 'em off till dark, an' then pull out fer camp. I'd have the best of 'em, me on shore an' them in the ford. That was the way I figured, anyway.

"Well, I hadn't got more'n halfway acrost when a slug whammed me up ag'inst the saddle horn. Got me in the side. Pike says it ain't bad, but it shore feels bad. I hung on an' looked back; the bang sounded closer'n I could account fer.

"Shore enough, there was Big Bill Longbow down on one knee at the south corner of the house, throwin' lead at me with his ole buffalo gun. He cut loose ag'in, an' got me in m' left arm, here. That time, I flopped off into the water—partly to make the old cuss think he got me, an' partly because I felt like floppin'. Hung onto a stirrup, though, an' let the roan haul me along.

"It was gittin' dusky by that time. Pore shootin' light, an' Longbow's too stingy t' waste lead. He quit shootin'. I didn't dast lift up enough to look back, but I could hear plain enough. You know how sound carries over water, specially when it's still as it was las' night.

"So I heard 'em gallop up to the store an' stop. An' I heard Bill Longbow holler at 'em 'fore they got there. I reckon they was headin' t' the ford, an' he hollered, an' then they swung over an' stopped at the store—I reckon that was how it was. I didn't dast look. I had t' keep down b'side the roan—"

His mind was fogging with the fever. Wylie leaned and touched his unhurt arm.

"What did Bill say, Kirk? You didn't tell us what it was he said when they rode up."

"Huh?" Kirk gave a slight start, looked at Wylie like a man roused from sleep. "Who? Big Bill, yuh mean? He hollered, 'It's all right, boys. I got 'im. Dropped 'im in the river.' There was more talkin' back an' forth—I didn't git what they said. I—I knowed about what they'd do next if they was smart."

"And what was that, Kirk?"

"Shoot m' horse. I knowed they'd do that. They'd make damn' shore he didn't git home. So I—worked ahead of 'im into a place where—where the hill made a shadow—up above the ford, kinda. They couldn't see me there. It shallows off fast, out f'm that rocky point. Somebuddy was crossin' over—I could hear 'im plain. I crawled up an' hid alongside a rock. An' he— he shot m' horse an' waited while it floated on down. An' he rode out an' looked at the bank—an' crossed back ag'in. I—I don't know where Steve went. I never seen 'im after that."

With a jerk of his head toward the door, Wylie gestured the Roman Four riders outside. Pike Stoddard brought his basin of brew, bullied Kirk into drinking a little. He lifted the blanket at the side, moistened the bandage with the mysterious concoction.

"Injun remedy," he explained succinctly to Wylie. "Keeps the fever down. But I got a big chaw of t'bacca on the wownd. Keeps out gangrene from settin' in."

"How did he get here, Pike?"

"Packed 'im in at daybreak. Comin' home from a big circle I rode last night, I run acrost him half a mile from the river. Tough, that feller. But he was about all in when I found 'im."

But that was not the thing uppermost now in Wylie's

mind. He looked thoughtfully at the Lightning boss.

"You've been in this country a heap longer than we have; didn't you know what kinda layout you had right across the river from you?" he asked bluntly.

"Can't say I did. Never had no truck with t'other side the river."

Wylie's shoulders lifted. "So I heard. Longbow managed to give you a pretty hard name, Pike, mostly hints. We've been losing cattle ever since we moved in here, and naturally we laid it to the Lightning. It did look that way. You always acted as if we had no business in this country, and if we could've got any evidence—but we couldn't. None against you, nor anyone else. Only, our stock kept disappearing. Funny your men never saw anything crooked going on."

"Well, they always left my stock alone," Pike answered. "The river was s'posed to be the boundary line, an' I never had a rep over there." Bitter lines settled about his thin, hard mouth. "If we didn't act friendly, it's because we're in the habit of goin' our own gait an' payin' no mind to neighbors. We had a pile uh trouble, few years back. We was plumb cured of bein' neighborly, long before you ever come into the country." He looked sharply at the other. "I reckon you heard about that."

His leathery old face saddened, and he went on without waiting for a reply:

"That was up on the Midas. There was a bunch come in there an' pertended to be nesters. Scattered up an' down the bottoms and started right in stealin' till we was near broke. They wasn't smooth as this bunch across the river. Barred an' blotched the Lightnin' and run their own brands over 'em—they didn't give a damn how coarse their work was. Thought, I reckon, that by hangin' in together they'd run us out.

"I warned 'em; made the rounds with about half the crew, and told 'em all the same thing—that they better git out 'fore they got in trouble. While we was on that job, some o' the first ones we visited hit straight for the ranch an' shot down my brother an' his son—all the kin I had in the world—right in our own c'rel. Wanted to show us what we was runnin' up ag'inst."

"That isn't the way we heard it," Wylie made laconic comment.

"No, I don't s'pose it is. They likely told yuh, though, what the outcome was. We cleaned 'em up. Like you'll have t' do with this gang, er pull stakes an' leave the country. They're all of 'em yeller—thieves always is cowards—and that cleanup we made on the Midas was a warnin' to all rustlers. They took it, too.

"We never had a word o' trouble over here. Dick Spellman come to work for me—I know now he was keepin' cases—but we never lost a hoof. Not," he amended dryly, "till after the Roman Four come in an' located."

"I—see. Playing one outfit against the other."

"That was the idee, I reckon. We begin to lose stock, big unbranded calves, mostly, but other stock too. We been losin' right along, an' it didn't look as if our new neighbors was goin' t' be any too desirable." He pulled down his mouth in a sour kind of grimace.

"Early this spring, we run onto some fellers workin' a bunch of stock, an' we started to ride up on 'em—wanted to make shore it was the IV. They stood us off with rifles, an' one uh my men got a bullet through his arm. Mind, you folks was plumb strangers. It looked t' me like you was out t' grab everything in sight. This jasper here, Kirk, was reppin' fer you. I sent 'im home, yuh remember. That was the time this shootin' our man was done.

"So we laid low an' waited t' see if you wouldn't git overbold an' tip yer hand. Dammit, I never s'spicioned it was the KM an' Block Diamond, rubbin' our ears an' sickin' us into a fight. I'm gittin' old, Brooks— but I ain't too old t' throw in with yuh an' clean that robbers' roost acrost the river. An' I got men in the Lightnin' outfit that shore knows how to go about doin' it!"

"Well, thanks, old timer. You're boss of this job: they'll know we mean business, with you in the lead."

"Don't forget Big Bill Longbow! He's the one that put me down on m' damn back right when I oughta be smokin' 'em up. Don't yuh pass him up, boss," Kirk implored weakly as they got to their feet.

"We don't pass nobody up. Come on, Brooks, le's git goin' b'fore they find out yore man here didn't float off down river."

Chapter Thirty-Three: MURDER ROUNDUP

As THE ROMAN FOUR COWBOYS roped fresh mounts from the Lightning remuda and led them out to the saddles, two dust-grimed figures rode around the corral into view, where they pulled up as if to get their bearings or to find familiar faces in the crowd.

Rock Sellers turned to look, then gave a whoop that

set his horse back on its haunches with amazement. Rock didn't care, even when the horse jerked loose and went stampeding out across the flat. Rock was loping over to the horsemen, yelling for Wylie Brooks to come see who was there.

Within a couple of minutes the two were surrounded by grinning Roman Four cowboys, Rock and Wylie close to the center. And yet there was little noise, and the Lightning men stood back and looked inquiringly at one another. In that country strangers were likely to be regarded with suspicion, and these two bore the mark of the long trail. Yet if they were known to the Roman Four, said the glances, they might be all right.

"We sure had one hell of a time getting you fellows located," the big heavy-set man, Len Moon, complained. "Where's Steve? By gosh, I got a crow to pick with him, the way he writes out directions. We bore northeast like he said, an' where did we land? In the roughest dang country God ever throwed away. This your spread, Wylie? Steve never said it was this close to the river. Don't jibe, somehow. Does it, Redneck?"

Telling those two what he had to tell them was the hardest task Wylie had ever been called upon to perform, and the most bitter. He made it short, mercifully blunt. Steve was dead, lying in his bunk waiting to be buried. Kirk was shot up, making a fight to live. Yes, they knew who done it, the same gang that had been stealing them blind since last fall. They were just going after them now—going to clean up the gang. The Lightning was going to help. And where were the trail herds? Turn the damn cattle loose, snapped Wylie. Let the boys heel themselves and come on. They would be needed.

Len Moon ripped out an ugly oath and swung down from his saddle. "Give me a fresh horse," he said grimly, "and I'll be back in an hour with a bunch uh boys that'll shore admire to git in an' make a hawg-killin' of them rustlers."

"Couldn't Rock or Sorry go?"

Len shook his head. "I orta be by m'self a while. I an' Steve—" He clamped his jaws hard and turned away.

A Lightning horse was forthcoming, and as if he were saddling against time in a relay race the big man changed his gear to the tall sorrel.

"Meet us on the main road to the ford!" Wylie called sharply at the last minute as Len was thrusting toe into stirrup.

He flung up his free hand, wheeled as if lifting the horse around on its hind feet, and was off, drawing a swirling billow of dust behind him as he rode. And until he vanished into the mouth of a gulch that led to the upper ridges they stood in silence and watched him go.

Well within the hour Len had allotted himself, thirty-six tight-lipped horsemen filed down to the ford and splashed in, rifles across their saddles, six-guns loosened in holsters, as implacable a cavalcade as ever crossed the Missouri on that old Whoop-up trail. Yet they sat their horses with a certain careless grace born of days spent in the saddle, month in, month out; young men, limber with youth; men whose slimness was the lean, tough-sinewed, enduring slenderness of middle age; big, fat-cushioned Len Moon; brick-red, freckled Davis, his partner; tall men, short men, middle-sized men—yet all alike when one looked at their grim faces and read there the purpose for which they rode.

They were not a mob, mouthing threats, yelling to one another to "string him up," and "hang the murderers"; they were all the more deadly because they rode almost in complete silence. A quiet sentence spoken now and then by those who took the lead: old Pike Stoddard and Wylie Brooks, Moon and Davis, Rock Sellers and a Lightning man; a muttered question and answer, asked and given between Roman Four riders with a year's separation to bridge when this job was finished.

Not a pleasant job, but one they sincerely believed was imperative. Certain fundamental laws of the land had been kicked aside for greed to ride rampant, and this must not be. In a country where the nation's industry had run ahead of its judicial machinery, law-abiding, honest men must see that the law was upheld. These three dozen wind-tanned, hard-riding, hard-lipped men were the law. They had to be, else there was no law in Kismet and the range it fed.

And Kismet looked the most inoffensive, insignificant spot in all Montana that warm forenoon. The half-breed who served Bill Longbow as choreman, clerk, or porter upon occasion reclined on elbows and shoulder blades, asleep on the porch, his weather-stained hat tilted over his face. In the barroom Big Bill and Dick Spellman yawned over a game of cribbage which they pegged with burned match stubs leaning askew from gimlet holes punched in a piece of two-by-four rough and unplaned. What conversation they held was of the game—the events of yesterday apparently thrust behind them as something over and done with, a danger averted and already half forgotten.

They looked up when spurred feet came clanking across the porch, but their eyes showed no alarm, merely a certain expectancy. True to his merchant soul, Big Bill Longbow laid down his cards and got up, sidling his huge body behind the bar, the wide grin of welcome spread across his face.

That grin stiffened, shrank slowly into his buttonhole mouth when he recognized his customers: Pike Stoddard and Wylie Brooks, two men he had never seen before, Rock Sellers and a Lightning man who hadn't crossed the river for months before. And still they came, with a clank and a shuffle of cowhide boot-soles and big rowels burring on the floor. More and more men, dribbling in as fast as they rode up and dismounted, the pasty-faced half-breed being pushed forward in their midst.

Dick Spellman knew. He showed it by the way his glance slid aside and darted this way and that, seeking escape from Pike Stoddard's bleak gray stare. His hands went up alongside his hatcrown and shook with a nervous palsy as he held them there, shook and winced as old Pike yanked the gun from Dick's holster and clouted him alongside the head with its barrel. It was not a felling blow, but Dick wilted into his chair and cowered there, panic in his light blue eyes that showed white eyeballs above the iris.

Big Bill Longbow was made of different mettle. Confederate of thieves and murderers, cold-blooded murderer himself (even though his latest attempt had not quite succeeded), he was no coward. The indomitable heart of a lion seemed to be implanted within his gross body. With the room full of men bent on vengeance, his little eyes had the cold malevolence of a cornered wild boar.

At the terse command to throw up his hands, Big Bill did not hesitate. He was standing behind the bar, hands down at his sides. As if dazed by the abrupt turn of affairs, his arms flexed at the elbows, then shot up with a gun in each hand, his cheek pushing back with the well-known Longbow grin.

At a distance of six feet, Rock Sellers shot him neatly between his fat-lidded piggish eyes. With a crash of breaking bottles he crumpled down behind the bar, dead before he could pull a trigger. The smell of spilled whisky tantalized the nostrils of men who had no time or thought for drinking liquor now.

"I'm playing Kirk's hand today," Rock said with hard satisfaction, and knocked the empty cartridge from his gun, calmly replacing it with a loaded shell. "Too bad I couldn't of drug it out long enough to tell 'im a few things."

There came an interruption; the swift, light steps of a woman running to see what was the meaning of that shot, Wylie instinctively knew. The door into the dining-room opened and banged shut, and Dolly Longbow stood in the barroom staring around at the strange faces, looking too for her father.

Dolly was a very pretty girl, with the dark, lustrous-eyed beauty which is often the heritage—one may say the compensation—of a white father and an Indian mother. She saw Big Bill's foot thrust out from behind the bar, read the significance of Dick Spellman's cowering passivity at the card table, swept again the relentless faces of the browned riders filling the room, and her head went up, eyes flashing with hate.

"What have you done to my father?" she demanded fiercely. "Who shot my father? Dick, you saw. Who did it?"

"Far as that goes, I did." Wylie swung on his heel and walked toward her. "No news to you, I reckon, that he shot Kirk Latimer in the back last night. You better go back into your own part of the house, Miss Longbow, and tell the squaw to stay outa sight. It won't be pretty around here for a while."

"I'll kill you for that, Wylie Brooks!" She took a step toward him, her hands half open and clenched like claws.

Dick Spellman raised his chin off his chest and looked fixedly at the girl. "You better do as they say, Dolly," he told her with gruff insistence. "Nothin' you can do—*here*. Go ahead. Pull out."

She opened her mouth to make some bitter retort, gave him a second intent, questioning look, then nodded.

"All right, Dick. I'll go." Her face paled. "Are you—are they—?"

"Go!" Dick half shouted. "Damn it, do what I tell yuh—*go!*"

She gave him one long look and turned away, swung back and faced them for a moment snarling like a trapped panther. "You—you *devils!*" she gritted under her breath, and fled, slamming the door behind her.

They heard her running to the back of the house, and a tension in the group relaxed.

Wylie was right, it was not going to be pretty.

Chapter Thirty-Four: DEATH WARRANT

ATTENTION TURNED AGAIN upon Dick Spellman, almost with palpable relief. Old Pike had pulled a small coil of rawhide from his pocket, moved in upon Dick.

"Stand up and put your hands behind yuh," he ordered in a quiet, grating voice, almost as if he were directing some small everyday task. Almost; that yard length of rawhide string hanging loosely from his hand gave a sinister meaning to the words, robbed them of all casualness. "One o' you boys might lend a hand here."

Two men stepped forward: Rock Sellers and Len Moon. Rock stooped mechanically and picked up a coat that had caught under his toe. He held it up, looked at it vacantly until his thoughts focused.

"Whose coat is this?" Not that it mattered much. But a man's mind will seize upon small things, dodging the crisis of events which he must face, or perhaps unconsciously giving himself a moment to rally his forces. "This yours, Spellman?"

More than one man noticed the start Dick Spellman gave. "Yes, dammit, you leave my coat alone!" he snapped, then bit his lip upon further speech.

Rock looked at him, looked at Pike and Wylie, turned the coat and felt for the inside pocket. "Secret tally book in here, yuh reckon?" he asked of no one in particular.

"If they is, it'll keep," Pike Stoddard flung over his shoulder.

But Rock was still looking at Dick Spellman, whose eyes could not seem to turn from the coat and whose face had gone ghastly with terror. "What's eatin' on yuh, Dick?" Rock asked with ironic solicitude. "You seem mighty anxious about this coat—and that's funny, too, seein' you won't be needin' it no more."

Grinning maliciously, he thrust a hand into the inside pocket, Dick watching him intently, for the moment ignoring the tying of his hands as Moon and old Pike pulled him to his feet. A tally book and stub of pencil the pocket yielded, and with them a creased envelope covered with pencil markings.

Rock glanced down at it, stiffened, and glared. He dropped the coat at his feet, whirled, and searched for Wylie with his eyes, holding up the envelope.

"Wylie, fer Godsake look at this! You know anything about it? Steve's. How'd Dick Spellman git aholt of it?"

Out of the crowd where he had been standing in muttered conference with Redneck Davis, Wylie Brooks pushed his way to Rock's side. He snatched the envelope, stared down at it, his face a pale mask of misery.

"Steve. He signed his own death warrant, sittin' in the shade right alongside me. And I sat there like a bump on a log and let him—never once dreamed—"

For this was the display of seemingly aimless markings, plain as daylight to a range man, showing all too clearly how Steve Tilton had worked out the answer to their losses:

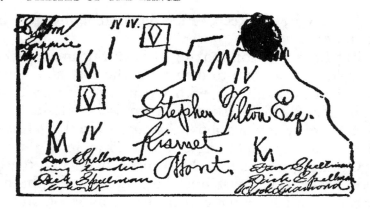

"You seen Steve workin' out them brands?" Len Moon's bellowing voice had sharpened as he stared over Wylie's shoulder. "You let these murderin' skunks git aholt of that? You musta bin crazy!"

"I didn't know what it was, Len." Wylie's voice shook. "It was just day before yesterday. Dave Spellman—cousin of this one here—was over at the ranch hunting horses, or so he said. We all sat in the shade of the cabin, and Steve was hunkered down paying no attention to us. He had that envelope (I know now that was the one) making marks on it. I knew he was figuring out something, and I let him alone.

"I reckon he threw away the envelope when he got up. He must have. I remember him tossing something into the weeds. Dave got hold of it, of course. Wait— his hat blew off." He looked up miserably into Moon's brooding face. "I didn't think anything about it at the time, but that's how Dave got hold of it. He knew right then the jig was up."

Len Moon took the envelope into his own hand, studied it briefly, and passed it on to Davis. "Simple.

So damn simple yuh'd hardly think they'd have the nerve. I reckon they banked on that."

"That, and the hard rep they gave the Lightning. And Dave would be the last man a fellow would suspect. Dick, here, is a Lightning man. He and Dave made out they hated each other."

"*Was* a Lightnin' man, yuh mean." Old Pike's jaw thrust outward. "C'm on, boys. Havin' a Judas in m' own outfit don't set none too good."

But Wylie stepped before him. "Just a minute! I want to know who shot Steve. Was it you, or Dave? Open up and tell who fired that shot!"

But Dick Spellman only pinched his mouth tighter and shook his head.

"No use wastin' time—we'll git 'em both, anyway. Them, an' all their gang. Come on, boys." Old Pike sent a bleak gray glance around the room and set in orderly motion their implacable purpose.

The confused shuffling of boots on the floor cleared, took the rhythmic tempo of marching feet as they moved to the door, out and across the platform, burred rowels down the steps. Only one man's feet lagged, shuffling along as if he were being half carried.

The barroom became very still, as still as the unsightly bulk of Big Bill Longbow, slumped down behind the bar with his porcine jowls wet with spilled whisky and blood.

Chapter Thirty-Five: BLOOD FOR BLOOD

LESS THAN TEN MINUTES LATER the grim cavalcade galloped down the trail that led to the KM headquarters.

From far up the river behind them the hoarse bellow of a steamer's whistle came booing down the wind: the *Golconda,* chugging down from Fort Benton, signaling Kismet for the landing.

Wylie turned and looked back at the small huddle of low buildings which was dignified with the official name of Kismet, and at the little steamer slowly swinging in to the crude landing to take on down-river mail. There would be no mail from Kismet today, he thought. Bill Longbow had not heard that whistle— nor had the long figure swinging gently from the big cottonwood alongside the trail from store to tiny wharf.

Glimpsing that idly turning object, Wylie shivered a little and faced to the front, thinking of how he had found Steve Tilton swinging like that, only that morning at daybreak. It seemed a week ago—a month almost; yet Steve still lay on his bed, worried no more about anything at all.

Wylie's face hardened. Down at the KM, over at the Block Diamond, or perhaps abroad somewhere hatching more deviltry, were men who still had a debt to pay with their own lives. Wherever they were, they would be hunted down; that debt must be collected without delay.

Pike Stoddard beside him pointed suddenly to a distant flurry of dust on the trail ahead. "Lookit that!" he grunted disgustedly. "Dolly Longbow, I betcha. Headed for the KM to pass the word to Dave. Oughta know'd better than to let that girl go off alone—but hell, I hated to make any more trouble 'n was necessary."

"I know; I thought the same thing, Pike. Hard

enough to lose her father and her sweetheart all of a sudden."

"Dick," said old Pike sourly, "might of thought he was ace-high with Dolly, but it was Dave she was stuck on. I'd oughta took that into consideration. She'd go hell-bent to warn Dave Spellman." He looked over his shoulder, then at Wylie. "We better hit the breeze. They'll scatter like quail—er gang up somewheres in ambush."

The scurrying dust disappeared into a coulee at least two miles away. At Pike's signal the posse leaned in their saddles and raced after that telltale dust. Above the drumming of hoofbeats they could hear the deep-toned blasts of the *Golconda's* whistle bellowing vainly at the Kismet landing. No doubt this was the first time since its river christening, thought Wylie, that the *Golconda* had arrived at an empty landing.

When they thundered down the coulee to the KM ranch, empty corrals and deserted cabins greeted them. Dolly Longbow's warning had evidently been heeded without argument or delay.

The Roman Four and the Lightning galloped on, leaving the crackle of flames behind them. The trail of the rustlers was plain in the long grass of the coulee bottom—there had been scant time to scatter, no time at all to cover their tracks. They were making straight for the Block Diamond, perhaps intending to give battle there.

Wylie hoped so. These men behind him were not to be cheated by craven flight. But the Block Diamond lay empty also and silent; and it too sent clouds of smoke and licking flames into the hot sunlight as they swept on. Across the neck of a huge bend in the river they galloped, their horses panting under the strain. Over a ridge, into a grassy hollow, and up another ridge they raced; and down the far slope they glimpsed their quarry, far ahead and riding furiously, while rounding the bend the *Golconda* chugged stolidly along, its broad stern wheel leaving a wide frothy wake behind it.

Down the hill at a breakneck pace they rode. The Roman Four and the Lightning riders slowly gaining on the Block Diamond and KM, and loosening the guns in their holsters or pulling rifles from saddle scabbards as they went. The river itself would halt the rustlers in a few minutes now, halt and hold them at bay until the posse came up. They were panic-stricken fools to come this way. They should have remembered, thought Wylie, how the bluffs closed in, a mile down the river bottom.

Then he saw that they were coming nearly opposite the flat across the river where that thieves' corral was hidden back among the trees. There must be a ford along here somewhere, a place where the stolen cattle had been taken across the river. It couldn't be below, for the river flowed flush with bold hills and cutbanks on this side. They must be going to cross. The fools! Didn't they know they could be picked off in the water like shooting ducks?

He turned to tell the others what they might expect, but at that moment Pike Stoddard twisted his scrawny body in the saddle and pointed.

"Yuh ketch onto their idee?" he shouted. "They're goin' t' hold up the boat an' make their getaway!

They'll do it, too, if you fellers don't wake up an' git a move on! C'm on, dammit, what yuh goin' t' sleep in yer saddles fer?"

Whereupon the posse plied quirts and spurs afresh and their lathered horses found some mysterious reserve of speed to give the chase. Minutes—seconds counted, now.

They were heading for a rough log landing halfway down the little flat, where the river boats swung in to load wood for their boilers. Wylie had not known of that boat landing—but now he saw that Pike had guessed correctly. The rustlers already were quitting their horses and scurrying behind the long ricks of cordwood piled at the shore end of the pier.

"Come *on!*" yelled old Pike furiously. "We got t' git in there ahead of that boat, you damn' lazy hounds—"

Already the *Golconda* was swinging in to the pier. Already Dolly Longbow was standing poised on the very last log, Dave Spellman beside her ready to swing her aboard and follow. A bell was clanging. Men were legging it down the landing, taking long leaps like scared antelope.

A rifle barked beside Wylie, and old Pike Stoddard gave a grunt of satisfaction as a man dropped in midstride. Other guns spoke. Len Moon, Redneck Davis, Rock Sellers forged up alongside Pike Stoddard and himself, tore past, riding wide lest they hamper the shooting, and firing as they rode.

The tired horses caught the excitement and there was no holding them now. They scattered a little without checking and raced forward in loose formation, black powder smoke floating in blobs behind them to mingle in an acrid cloud.

Wylie Brooks fired, loaded, fired again. Dave Spellman was fighting—he was glad of that. In his heart there was an ache for a friendship broken, a trust betrayed. He was glad Dave had courage, even though he hoped his own bullet would be the one that killed Dave.

But there, down on her knees and sighting across the steamer's rail, fought Dolly Longbow. Dave was behind her—and was that courage, to stand behind a pile of dried hides on the deck and fight, while Dolly knelt beside the rail? On the river bank Wylie flung himself from his horse and took careful aim. But even as his finger was squeezing the trigger he saw Dave Spellman crumple down. His bullet zipped across the deck a shade too late; he didn't know whether he was sorry for that or glad.

The *Golconda* was backing out as precipitately as possible into the river, her captain evidently not caring much for flying lead. From the pile of hides other shots came viciously, and behind the cordwood pile a reluctant rear guard fought for their lives, a losing battle, as they must have known from the start. For when lawlessness and murder come to hand grips with outraged decency and justice, in the end right does prevail, though it is doubtful if any KM or Block Diamond man gave that angle so much as a passing thought.

"It looks as though we got all of the gang but Dolly on board the boat," Wylie said shakenly when the *Golconda* had kicked herself out of range around the jutting banks below the flat. "If someone—"

"Job ain't done yit," snapped Pike Stoddard. "Boys

over there are collectin' some tree trimmin's from behind that woodpile. Yuh shore Dave Spellman got his ticket?"

"Through ticket to hell. What's the matter, Pike? You hurt?"

"No-o, none t' speak of. Somebuddy nicked me in m' gun arm an' sp'iled my shootin'. Some o' the boys is worse off 'n I am, I reckon." He spat away from the wind into the sand of the river bank and looked at Wylie with a quizzical squint in his eyes. "You got some good men, Brooks. Most as good as the Lightnin'."

They borrowed a wagon from the man who supplied wood for the steamers and lived back in a little draw, and hauled four wounded men as tenderly as the rough trail would permit back to the Lightning. But they left three KM rustlers and two Block Diamond men swinging from cottonwood branches, and of the rest they doubted whether a man escaped. Two of their own dead—both riders from the south, as it happened—were buried hastily in one grave, shrouded only in their saddle blankets and without benefit of clergy.

Later, the remainder of the Roman Four and Lightning riders combed the country north of the river and gathered what stolen cattle had not already been sold. It was a hard task and it wore thin the tempers and sometimes snapped the patience of the men. But friendships were made between the two outfits that would endure as long as they lived to ride the range.

Roman Four cattle and Lightning cattle grazed side by side thereafter. A New Englander with a large family took over the store, saloon, and post office at Kismet, and soon a small village clustered there at the ford. There was talk of a schoolhouse, and some speculation among the cowboys over the romantic possibilities of having a schoolma'am within riding distance on a fine Sunday afternoon.

One element common to range life was totally absent from that country, however, and that was cattle thieves and killers—an element which could think of no inducement whatever for risking the vengeance of Pike Stoddard and those hard-riding, fast-shooting men of the Roman Four.